DANTE'S UNEXPECTED LEGACY

DANTE'S UNEXPECTED LEGACY

BY

CATHERINE GEORGE

First published in Great Britain 2014
by Mills & Boon, an imprint of Harlequin (UK) Limited,
Large Print edition 2014
Eton House, 18-24 Paradise Road,
Richmond, Surrey, TW9 1SR

© 2014 Catherine George

ISBN: 978-0-263-24118-1

Harlequin (UK) Limited's policy is to use papers that
are natural, renewable and recyclable products and made
from wood grown in sustainable forests. The logging
and manufacturing processes conform to the legal
environmental regulations of the country of origin.

Printed and bound in Great Britain
by CPI Antony Rowe, Chippenham, Wiltshire

This one's for Justin

CHAPTER ONE

ROSE SAT RIGIDLY, every nerve on edge as the plane took off. No turning back now. For years she'd been turning down invitations to Florence, flatly refusing to be parted from her little daughter, or to take her child with her. But this time refusal had been impossible.

'Please, *please* come,' Charlotte had begged. 'Just you and me in a luxury hotel for a couple of days. God knows you can do with a break, and I'll pay for everything and send you a plane ticket, so absolutely no expenses on your part. You know Bea will be fine with your mother, so don't say no this time. I really need you, Rose. So come. Please!' she'd added, and because Charlotte was her oldest and closest friend and she loved her like a sister, Rose had finally given in.

'Oh, all right. If it means that much to you I will. But why a hotel and not your place?'

'I want you all to myself.'

'Fabio can't be cool about this. It's your wedding anniversary, isn't it?'

'He'll be away for it on some business trip,' said Charlotte miserably. 'Besides, he doesn't know about the hotel yet. But I've already booked, so there's nothing he can do about it—not that he would, of course.'

Rose wasn't so sure. A possessive husband like Fabio Vilari would surely be anything but cool if his wife took a hotel break in Florence without him, even if it was with her lifelong friend and the bridesmaid at their wedding. But from the moment Rose had said a reluctant yes to the trip Charlotte rang every day to make sure that she hadn't changed her mind, and in her final call sprang a surprise with instructions to take a taxi from Santa Maria Novella railway station to the hotel. 'I'll meet you there later in time for dinner, Rose. I can't wait!'

Money, if the hotel brochure was anything to go by, was obviously not part of Charlotte's problem, but if something was going wrong with her marriage Rose couldn't see what earthly help a single parent like herself could give her friend, other than to provide a sympathetic ear. Still, the note of tearful desperation in her friend's voice had been so worrying that Rose had enlisted her mother's willing help, covered her child's face with kisses and made for Heathrow with her shoulder ready for Charlotte to cry on.

On terra firma in Pisa Airport, Rose concentrated on collecting her luggage and finding the train for Florence, but once she'd boarded it the Tuscan scenery passed her by almost unnoticed in her worry about possible problems left behind and the all-too-probable ones awaiting her at journey's end. Her daughter was used to spending time with her beloved gramma while Rose went out to work, but Mummy had always been home before bedtime. Rose blinked hard. The thought of her darling Bea crying for her in the night was unbearable. Yet Charlotte had been there for Rose through thick and thin in the past, and now her friend was the one needing help and support for once Rose had no option but to get to her as quickly as possible to provide it.

Rose came to with a start as the train pulled into Santa Maria Novella and was soon wheeling her suitcase through the heat and bustle of the crowds streaming from the lofty station into the late afternoon Florentine sunshine, so very different from the cool mists left behind. The taxi driver who eventually picked her up took a look at her hotel brochure and whisked her on a fast, chaotic drive past tall old buildings in narrow streets filled with honking cars and scooters en route to the banks of the River Arno. Rose stared, impressed, when they reached the hotel. Charlotte was certainly pushing the boat out for her. A flight of stone steps with a red carpet runner led up to an arched doorway crowned by a fabulous Venetian glass fanlight. Rose paid the driver, wishing she'd worn something more elegant than denim jeans and jacket for her red carpet entrance as she trailed her suitcase past marble statues and urns of flowers in the vaulted foyer. She approached the man behind the reception desk at the foot of a sweeping staircase and gave him her name.

'Buonasera,' he said courteously, but to her relief continued in English. 'Welcome to Florence, Miss Palmer. If you will just sign the register? I am to inform you that Signora Vilari has ordered dinner for two in the hotel restaurant this evening.'

Rose smiled gratefully. 'Thank you.'

'*Prego*. If you require anything at all, please ring. Enjoy your stay.'

A porter took charge of the luggage to escort Rose to a lift rather like an ornate brass birdcage. It took them up two floors at such a leisurely rate she could have walked up faster, but she was utterly delighted when she reached her room. She tipped the porter and went straight out onto a balcony looking down on the River Arno, her feelings a heady mix of trepidation and excitement as she recognised the sun-gilded bridge farther upstream as the famous Ponte Vecchio. She was actually, unbelievably, here in Florence at last. She sent a text to Charlotte to confirm her arrival, and then rang her mother.

'No problems, darling; Bea's as happy as a lark,' Grace Palmer assured her. 'She's playing with Tom in the garden before her bath. Do you want to speak to her?'

'I just long to, Mum, but I won't in case it upsets her. If she's happy let's keep her that way.'

'She'll be fine. You know we'll take good care of her, so for heaven's sake, relax and enjoy yourself.'

Rose promised to try, said there was no news

from Charlotte yet, but would report tomorrow. She chose a tonic from the minibar and sat back on one of the reclining chairs on the balcony to breathe in the scents and sounds of Florence as she watched the traffic stream past across the river. For the first time in for ever at this time of day she had absolutely nothing to do—but missed her child too much to enjoy it. *Stop it*, she told herself irritably. Now she was here it was only sensible to make the most of her short break in this beautiful city. But what on earth was going on with Charlotte and Fabio? Could Fabio be cheating on her? Rose glowered. In the unlikely event that she ever acquired a husband herself her gut reaction would be grievous bodily harm if the man started playing away. She checked her silent phone again, took a last look at the sparkling waters of the Arno and went inside to soak in the bath for as long as she liked for once.

With still no word from Charlotte, the uneasiness grew as Rose got ready for the evening. To keep occupied, she took longer over her appearance than she ever had time for normally and even coaxed her newly washed hair into an intricate up-do. She nodded at her reflection in approval. Not bad. Her long-serving little black dress looked pretty good now she'd lost a pound or two. Charlotte's clothes were always wonderful, courtesy of a wealthy, besotted husband—Rose bit her lip, wondering if there lay the problem. Maybe Fabio Vilari was no longer so besotted. Or, worst scenario of all, was now besotted with someone else.

She leapt away from the mirror as the phone rang. At last!

'Hello,' she said eagerly, but her face fell at the news that a letter had arrived for her.

A *letter*?

'Thank you. I'll come down for it right away.' And wait for Charlotte downstairs with a drink.

Too impatient to wait for the lift, Rose hurried down the imposing staircase as fast as she could in her kept-for-best heels and crossed the foyer to the reception desk. The bulky envelope, addressed in Charlotte's unmistakable scrawl, was handed to her, along with the information that the gentleman who'd delivered it wished to speak with her.

'*Buonasera*, Rose,' said a voice behind her. 'Welcome to Firenze.'

Her heart, which had taken a nosedive at the

sight of Charlotte's handwriting, flew up to hammer Rose in the ribs. To hide her horrified reaction, she turned very slowly to confront a tall, slim man with dark curling hair and a face that could be straight out of a Raphael portrait. A face she had never forgotten, though heaven knew she had tried. Here in the handsome, irresistible flesh was her reason for refusing all invitations to Tuscany—to avoid meeting up with her daughter's father again.

'Good heavens—Dante Fortinari,' she said lightly when she could trust her voice. 'What a surprise!'

'A pleasant one, I hope?' He took her hand, a light in his blue eyes that made her want to turn tail and run. 'I am so very happy to see you again, Rose. Will you have a drink while you read your letter?'

Her first reaction was to refuse point-blank and tell him to get lost, but after a pause she nodded warily. 'Thank you.'

'Come.' He led her to a table in the hushed sophistication of the lounge bar. 'You would like wine?'

She felt in crying need of something even stronger than wine after the shock of seeing him again, but to keep her wits about her opted for water. 'Sparkling water, please. Will you excuse me while I read this?'

Dante Fortinari gave the order to a waiter then sat watching intently while she read her letter. Rose Palmer had changed in the years since their last meeting at Charlotte Vilari's wedding over four years ago. Then she had been an innocent just past her twenty-first birthday, but now she was very much a woman. Hair still the colour of *caramello* was swept up in a precarious knot that made his fingers yearn to bring it tumbling down. Combined with the severe dress, it gave her a look of sophistication very different from his memory of her. His mouth twisted. She had been so irresistible in her happiness for her friend that day, but the carefree young bridesmaid had now matured into a poised, self-contained adult who was very obviously not pleased to see him. This was no surprise. He had half expected her to snatch her letter and walk away, refusing to talk to him at all.

Rose, in the meantime, was reading Charlotte's note in dismay.

You'll want to hit me, love, when you read this—I don't blame you one bit. Fabio woke me up yesterday morning with flowers, a gorgeous gold bracelet, plus tickets for a surprise trip to New York for today of all days.

God, Rose, the relief was enormous. I came across the tickets and hotel reservation by accident a while ago and immediately pole-vaulted to the wrong conclusion—that Fabio was taking someone else and pretending it was a business trip. And on our wedding anniversary! That was why I needed you so badly.

Sorry to be such a drama queen—I've been a total idiot. I was about to ring you to grovel and cancel your trip when Fabio insisted a little holiday would be very good for you after all your efforts to get away. I agreed wholeheartedly, so take it easy, Rose, and enjoy a taste of la dolce vita *before you fly back. Lord knows you deserve it.*

Enclosed is some spending money for meals and shopping—and Fabio says don't dare refuse it or he'll be very hurt.

*Buy presents, if nothing else. I'll fly over
to catch up very soon.
Love always, Charlotte.*

'Bad news?' asked Dante.

Rose gave him a dazed look. 'I flew here to meet Charlotte for a little holiday, but Fabio's taken her on a surprise trip to New York today instead.' She smiled valiantly to mask her crushing disappointment. 'Never mind. I've always wanted to visit Florence.'

'But in company with your friend, not alone.' Sympathy gleamed in the vivid blue eyes that had haunted her dreams and given her many a disturbed night in the past. Not that she was ever short of those in the present.

Rose shrugged philosophically. 'I'd prefer that, of course, but I certainly won't lack something to do in a city like Florence. I'll explore as many museums and galleries as possible, enjoy glorious meals and gaze into shop windows as much as I like.' And even swallow her pride and spend some of the money sent with the letter.

'But all that is for tomorrow. Tonight, it is time to dine. Charlotte has made a dinner reservation for two here tonight.' Dante reached across to touch her hand. '*Allora*, since she cannot join you, it would give me much pleasure to take her place.'

Rose snatched her hand away. 'Will you bring your wife along, too?'

'*Cosa?*' He sat back, his eyes suddenly arctic. 'You forget. I no longer have a wife.'

Rose winced. Had his wife *died*? 'I…I apologise. I didn't know.'

He raised a cynical eyebrow. 'Charlotte did not tell you that Elsa left me?'

'No.'

'You surprise me! In Fortino it was such a hot topic of conversation I was grateful when my travels took me to the vineyards of California for a while.' He drained his glass. 'But now you know I am *solo* again, and have been for years, may I have the honour of your company at dinner tonight, Miss Palmer?'

She studied him in silence. Her first instinct was to refuse. But she was secretly daunted by the thought of dining alone in such opulent and formal surroundings. Even so, after refusing for years to come to Italy in case she ran into Dante Fortinari again, it would be wiser to have some food sent to her room rather than accept the company of the man who'd caused total upheaval in her life after their first and only meeting. Her brain, which was still furious with him, ordered her to refuse point-blank, but her heart, the unruly organ which had got her into trouble in the first place, was urging her to forget wisdom for once. And, idiot that she was, that was what she was going to do. She would never come here again, so what harm in making use of him?

'You are taking much time to decide, Rose,' Dante pointed out. 'Do you wish for my company or not?'

'Yes. Thank you.' She eyed him curiously. 'How did you get involved in acting as delivery boy for Charlotte?'

He shrugged. 'Fabio offered to deliver a package to a friend of mine in New York and Charlotte requested a favour in return. I was most happy to do this because it meant meeting you again, Rose.' He signalled to a waiter for some menus.

'But do you have a place here in Florence these days? I vaguely remember that you lived in the family home at the Fortinari vineyards.'

'I did at one time, but now I own a house a few

kilometres from our vineyards at Fortino. Now my father is retired I help run the business with my brother, Leo. He is maestro of production; I am good at the selling,' Dante said without conceit.

No need to tell her that. 'You came a long way just to deliver a letter.'

'A trip to Firenze is always a pleasure,' he assured her, and held her eyes very deliberately. 'Also, I wanted very much to see you again.'

'I'm surprised you even remembered me after all this time,' she said tartly.

'I have never forgotten you, Rose,' he assured her, and for the first time gave her the bone-melting smile that had caused all the trouble in the first place. *'Allora*, what do you like to eat?'

'Practically anything I don't have to cook myself!'

He eyed her over the top of his menu. 'You live alone?'

'No. I share a house not far from my mother.'

'I remember her well—a very lovely lady who looks much too young to be your mother.'

'That she does.' Rose returned to her menu. 'What do you recommend?'

'If you like fish the salmon will be good here. Or there is the *bistecca alla Fiorentina*, the famous steak of the region. You have travelled a long way today, Rose; you must be hungry.'

'I am, but not enough to attempt a steak. I'll have the salmon.' Her stomach was in such knots that she was sure she'd only be able to manage a bite or two at the most.

Rose listened as he gave the order to the waiter, wishing she could understand the rapid, melodious interchange. She had once fancied learning Italian to add to her schoolgirl French, but studies of a different kind had taken up all her time.

Later, experiencing the effortless service Charlotte had described, Rose was glad of Dante's company among the elegantly dressed diners. She would have felt uncomfortable dining alone. Instead, now she was over the first shock of meeting up with him again, she enjoyed the ravioli in sage-fragrant butter sauce Dante insisted she try for a first course, and ate her share of the exquisite little vegetables served with their main course. But she kept firmly to water instead of the wine he offered.

'You drank champagne the first time we met,'

Dante reminded her. 'You were such a delight in that charming dress.'

'It was a long time ago,' she said coolly.

'You do not remember the occasion with pleasure?'

Her eyes clashed with his. 'Of course I do. It was Charlotte's wedding day. She was on cloud nine and I had just left university with a respectable degree. Euphoria all round.'

He held the look in silence for a moment then got up to escort her to the bar. 'Will you take a little cognac with your coffee?'

'Since I abstained over dinner, I will, please.' Rose needed some kind of stimulant for once. A sip of the fiery spirit helped her to relax a little as she looked across at her companion. Now she could study him objectively without wanting to hit him, he looked a lot older and harder-edged than the effervescent charmer who'd made Charlotte's wedding so memorable for the bridesmaid. There had been other young Italian men among Fabio's relatives and friends at the wedding, but Dante had monopolised Rose so completely she'd had no eyes for anyone else.

'You are very quiet,' he observed.

'It's been a very eventful day.'

'So tell me all about your life, Rose.'

'I run a bookkeeping business from home.'

His eyebrows rose. 'You did not take up your career in accountancy?'

'No, though the qualifications come in very handy in my line of business.' She changed the subject. 'Dante, I know it's a bit late to say this, but I was very sorry about your grandmother.'

'*Grazie*. I miss her very much.'

'Do you miss your wife, too?'

'No. Not at all.' His eyes hardened. 'The marriage was a bad mistake. When Elsa soon left me for another man my brother said I should thank God for such good fortune. Leo was right.'

Rose looked him in the eye. 'Odd you forgot to mention Elsa when we first met.'

His mouth twisted. 'I did not forget. I refused to let thoughts of her spoil my time with you. I was very angry because she refused to cancel a fashion shoot to accompany me to Fabio's wedding.'

'So you made do with me.'

'No! This is not true, Rose. I took great delight in your company.' His eyes held hers. 'Am I too late to apologise for leaving you so suddenly?'

'I completely understood when I heard that your grandmother had died.' She held the brilliant blue gaze steadily. 'Not so much when I was told about Elsa.'

His jaw clenched as he beckoned to a waiter. 'I need more cognac. Will you join me?'

'No, thanks.' She got up. 'I'm a bit tired, Dante, so—'

'No!' He sprang up. 'It is early yet. Stay a little longer with me, Rose, *per favore.*'

Since only sheer pride had forced her to make the first move, she nodded graciously and sat down again, eyeing Dante's glass. 'Should you be drinking that before a long drive?'

'I am not driving. I have reserved a room here at the hotel tonight so that I can be your guide to the city tomorrow.'

Rose stiffened. 'Charlotte asked you to do this?'

'No, she did not. It was my idea.' He lifted a shoulder, his eyes cold again. '*Non importa*, if you do not desire my company I will leave in the morning.'

That would be the best move all round, as Rose knew only too well. But she was a stranger in a city foreign to her and didn't speak a word of

Italian, so it was only practical to take advantage of someone native to the place. After all the trouble he'd caused her, he might as well make himself useful.

'I'd appreciate your services as guide, Dante. Thank you.'

'It is my great pleasure, Rose!' He reached across the table to touch her hand, eyes warm again. 'I will try to make your stay memorable.'

He wouldn't have to try hard. In spite of her initial rage at the sight of him, it had taken only a minute in Dante's company again to remember how easy it had been to fall in love with him all those years ago. He'd been a charming, attentive companion who'd shown unmistakable signs of returning her feelings on Charlotte's wedding day, which had made it all the more devastating when she'd learned about his missing fiancée after he'd gone. In sick, outraged reaction to the blow, she had immediately blanked him out of her mind and pretended she'd never met him. And because she'd flatly refused to listen whenever his name came up, Charlotte had eventually given up mentioning him. Yet Charlotte had sent Dante to the hotel with her letter. Rose made a note to have words with Signora Vilari on the subject next time they spoke.

She took her hand away. 'Won't it be boring for you, Dante, showing me round a city you know so well?'

He shook his head. 'Firenze will seem new to me, seen through your eyes. But why have you not been here before, Rose? I had hoped so much to see you again when you visited Charlotte, but you never came.'

'Too much work to get away. And I see her regularly when she comes to visit her father.'

'She told me Signor Morley shares his life with your mother. You are happy with this?'

Rose nodded. 'It's a happy arrangement all round.'

'It was plain that you were all close at the wedding. I am fortunate to possess both my parents, but no longer, alas, my grandmother. I adored her and miss her still.' Dante's eyes lit with sudden heat. 'Only the message telling me she was dying could have torn me away from you so suddenly that night, you understand? But, *grazie a Dio*, because I left immediately I arrived at the Villa Castiglione in good time to say goodbye to

Nonna and hold her hand in mine before she... she left us.'

'I'm glad of that,' said Rose quietly. Though at the time she hadn't believed a word of it, convinced the call had been from some girlfriend—a theory which had seemed proved beyond all doubt next morning when she found out about Elsa.

'Nonna left her house to me.' Dante's eyes darkened. 'At first I did not want the Villa Castiglione, afraid I would miss her there too much. But because it was Nonna's greatest wish my parents persuaded me to live there.'

'Alone? You've found no replacement for Elsa yet?'

'No.' He arched a wry black eyebrow. 'You think such a thing is easy for me?'

'I don't think about you at all.' She shrugged. 'After all, I only met you once.'

His eyes narrowed to an unsettling gleam. 'And you did not look back with pleasure on that meeting!'

'Oh, yes, most of it. I had a great time with you all day. But once I knew you were spoken for I never gave you another thought.' She smiled sweetly and got to her feet. 'Now I really must go to bed.'

He walked with her to the ornate lift. 'I shall take much pleasure in our tour of Firenze, Rose.'

'You must tell me what to see.'

'When do you fly home?'

'Thursday morning.'

'So soon!' He frowned. 'But that gives you only one day for the sightseeing. We must meet early for breakfast.'

'I thought I'd have it sent up—'

'No, no.' Dante shook his head imperiously. 'I will take you to breakfast in the Piazza della Signora to begin on the sightseeing as we eat. We shall meet down here at nine, *d'accordo*?'

Rose nodded. 'I'll enjoy the luxury of a lie-in for once.'

'You rise early for your work?'

'Much too early.' She smiled politely as the lift glided to a halt and pressed the button for her floor. 'Which one for you?'

'The same.' He showed her his room number. 'So if you are nervous in the night you can call me and I will come.'

Rose shot him an arctic look. 'Not going to happen, Dante.'

'Che peccato!' When they reached her room, Dante opened the door and stood aside with a bow. 'Now lock your door to show me you are safe.'

Rose nodded formally. 'Thank you for your company this evening, Dante.'

His lips twitched. 'Because it was better than none?'

Rose let her silence speak for her as she closed and locked the door.

Dante made for his room and went out onto his balcony, deep in thought as he stared down at the Arno. Rose Palmer was very different now from the girl he'd fallen more and more in love with as the hours passed during that memorable day. Even in the rush to reach his grandmother's side, and the searing grief that followed, it had been impossible to stop thinking of the girl he'd been forced to abandon so suddenly that night. He had made a vow to apologise to Rose in person when she first visited the Vilaris. But she never came and the apologies were never made.

It was no surprise that she had been hostile at

first tonight. Whereas he had felt a great leap of his heart at the first sight of her, and an urgent need to offer comfort when she found Charlotte wasn't joining her. He had seized the chance to propose his own company instead. He smiled sardonically, well aware that Rose had accepted the offer only because it was marginally preferable to spending her brief time in Florence alone. Tomorrow, therefore, he must do everything in his power to make her stay pleasurable before she went back to her bookkeeping. He shook his head in wonder. Could she not do something more interesting with her life?

Convinced, for a variety of reasons, that she'd lie awake all night, Rose fell asleep the instant she closed her eyes. When she opened them again the room was bright with early sunshine, and with a gasp she shot upright to grab her phone, and smiled in relief when she saw a message from her mother. Grace Palmer had come late to the skills of texting, and the message was brief:

Everything fine. Have lovely day.

Reassured, Rose sent off a grateful response and then stretched out in the comfortable bed, feeling rested after the surprise of the best night's sleep she'd had for ages. Eventually, she wrapped herself in the hotel robe and went out on the balcony, face uplifted to the sunshine. Since she *was* here at last, doing the last thing she'd expected to do, pride urged her to make herself as presentable as possible now Dante Fortinari was to be her guide.

In the years since she'd last seen him she'd persuaded herself he couldn't possibly be as gorgeous as she remembered. And she was right. Now Dante was in his early thirties maturity had added an extra dimension to his dark good looks—something her wilful hormones responded to even while the rest of her disapproved. So since a capricious fate—or Charlotte—had brought them together again, she would make use of his escort for a day and then tomorrow, back home in the real world, erase him from her life. Once again.

Dante had worn a suit cut by some Italian master of the craft the evening before, so if he'd decided to stay on the spur of the moment it seemed likely he'd have to wear the same thing again today. With that in mind, Rose went for pink cotton jeans instead of the denims worn for travelling. With a plain white cotton tee, small gold hoops in her ears and her hair caught back with a big tortoiseshell barrette, she slid her feet into the flats brought for sightseeing with Charlotte and felt ready to take on the day.

Dante was waiting in the foyer when she went downstairs shortly before nine, his look of gleaming appreciation worth all her effort. '*Buongiorno*, Rose. You look delightful!'

So did Dante. She raised an eyebrow at his pale linen trousers and crisp blue shirt. 'Thank you. You've been shopping?'

He shook his head. 'It is my custom to keep a packed bag in the car.'

Her lips twitched. 'Ready for unexpected sleepovers?'

He grinned, looking suddenly more like the youthful Dante she remembered. 'You are thinking the wrong thing, *cara*. I do this to impress the clients. Here in Italy, image is everything.' He looked at her feet with approval. '*Bene*, you are prepared for walking.'

'Always.' As they left the hotel she looked at the sparkling river in delight. 'Though my daily walks at home are in rather different surroundings from these.'

'But the town you live in is a pleasant place, yes?'

She nodded. 'Still, it's good to take a short break from it. My only time away from home before was in university.'

'I remember your pleasure at doing well in your final exams, and the celebrations which followed them.' He frowned as they began to walk. 'But you did not continue with the accountancy.'

'No, I didn't.' She waved a hand at the beautiful buildings they were passing. 'So talk, Signor Guide. Give me names to go with all this architecture.'

Dante obliged in detail as they walked with the river on one side and tall, beautiful old buildings on the other. But eventually he steered Rose away from the Arno to make for the Piazza della Signora with its dominant fifteenth century Palazzo Veccio that still, Dante informed her, served as Town Hall to Florence. He steered her past the queues for the famous Uffizi Gallery and the statues in the Loggia dei Lanzi on their way to the Caffe Rivoire. 'You may look at all the sculpture you wish later,' he said firmly and seated her at an outdoor table with a view of the entire Piazza. 'But now we eat.'

Rose nodded. 'Whatever you say. Breakfast is a rushed affair at home, so I shall enjoy this.' In the buzz of this sunlit square packed with people—and pigeons—she could hardly fail. She sat drinking it all in to report on later.

'I will buy you a guidebook so that you may show your mother what you have seen,' said Dante as the waiter brought their meal. 'You will take orange juice?'

'Thank you.' As she sipped, her eyes roved over the statuary she could see everywhere, and felt a sudden stab of envy for the man sitting so relaxed beside her.

'That is a very cold look you give me,' commented Dante, offering a plate of warm rolls.

'I was thinking how privileged you are to live in a place like this. You probably take all this wonderful sculpture for granted.'

'Not so. I do not live in the city,' he reminded her. 'Therefore, I marvel at it every time I return. And, Signorina Tourist, these statues were erected for more than decoration. The big white Neptune in the fountain with his water nymphs commemorates ancient Tuscan naval victories.'

'How about the sexy Perseus brandishing Medusa's severed head over there? Just look at those muscles!'

Dante laughed, his eyes dancing at the look on her face. 'He is a Medici warning to enemies, while the replica of Michelangelo's *David* represents Republican triumph over tyranny.' He shook his head. 'Enough of the lessons. What would you like to do next?'

'Could we just sit here for a while, Dante?' Rose refused to feel guilty because she was enjoying herself so much. She could go back to resentment and hostility later.

'Whatever you wish.' He beckoned to a waiter for more coffee.

Rose tensed as her phone beeped; she read the text, replied to it quickly and put the phone away. 'Sorry about that—one of my clients.' She smiled radiantly at the waiter who topped up her cup. *'Grazie.'*

'Prego!' The man returned her smile with such fervour Dante frowned.

'It is good I am here with you,' he said darkly when they were alone.

'Why?'

'To keep my beautiful companion safe from admirers.'

Rose shook her head impatiently. 'Hardly beautiful—I'm just reasonably attractive when I make the effort.' But sometimes the effort was hard.

'You are far more than just attractive, Rose,' he said with emphasis, and signalled to the offending waiter. 'I will pay, and then we shall see more of Firenze.'

'Dante,' she said awkwardly, 'could I pay, please?'

He stared at her in blank astonishment. *'Cosa?'*

She felt her colour rise. 'You've given up your time to show me round. I can't expect you to feed me as well.'

'It is my privilege,' he said, looking down his nose. 'Also a great pleasure.'

'But I feel I'm imposing.'

Dante shook his head. 'You are not.' He took her hand and stayed close enough to make himself heard as they threaded their way through the crowds in the Piazza. 'I was forced to rush away from you last time, Rose, with only a brief apology. This time perhaps you will think better of me after we say goodbye tomorrow.'

Less likely to murder him, certainly. 'When you've been so kind, how could I not?' she said lightly. She stood looking up in wonder as they reached Perseus and his grisly trophy. 'Wow! I've seen Renaissance art in books but the bronze reality is something else entirely.'

'Cellini was a master,' he agreed, and moved on to the next, graphic sculpture. 'So was Giambologna, yes? You like his *Rape of the Sabine Women*? It is carved from a single block of marble, but it is flawed, as you see.'

Rose wrinkled her nose. 'I'm not so keen on that one.'

'Then let us go to the Bargello, which was once a prison, but now houses sculpture. Donatello's bronze *David* from a century earlier is there. You will like that, I think. Then you cannot leave Firenze without a visit to the Accademia to gaze in wonder at the greatest statue of all—the marble *David* by Michelangelo.'

Rose found that Dante was right when they arrived at the rather forbidding Bargello. On the upper loggia, it needed only one look at Donatello's jaunty David, nude except for stylish hat and boots, for Rose to fall madly in love. She turned to Dante, her eyes bright with recognition. 'I've seen him before on a television programme.' She grinned. 'The handsome lady in charge of his restoration couldn't help smoothing his bottom!'

He laughed, his eyes alight as he squeezed her hand. 'You have not changed so much after all, *bella*. But now you must have a *tramezzini* and a drink. We may have to wait for some time in the Accademia.'

She shook her head. 'I don't need anything yet after all that breakfast, Dante. Let's go now.'

As Dante had forecast, at the Academy of Fine Arts they had quite a wait among throngs of tourists with cameras and students with backpacks, but when they finally gained entrance to the star attraction Rose stood motionless in pure wonder at the sight of the monumental white figure gazing sternly far above their heads, the sling he would use to kill Goliath at the ready over one shoulder.

'You are impressed?' murmured Dante in her ear.

'How could I not be?' With reluctance, she dragged her eyes from the statue. 'Thank you so much for bringing me here.'

'It is my pleasure as much as yours, Rose. But

now, if you have looked at David long enough, we shall go in search of food. Shall we go back to Caffe Rivoire, or would you like to try a different place?'

'The Rivoire again, but just coffee and a snack, please.'

'You shall have whatever your heart desires.'

CHAPTER TWO

To Dante's amusement Rose took surreptitious glances at her phone from time to time when they were seated among the greenery at a table close to the building, a little away from the press of crowds and pigeons in the Piazza.

'You are expecting a call from your lover?' he demanded at last.

'Sorry. Just checking for any client problems,' she lied. No way was she telling him she was checking on her child—who just happened to be his daughter. She thrust the phone in her bag, feeling suddenly cold. Would Dante try to lay claim to Bea if he found out about her? No way was she sharing her child with him. Bea was hers and hers alone.

'You look tense. Forget the work for today,' commanded Dante. 'Let us enjoy this unexpected gift of time together. First you must rest for a while in your room and then later we shall go wherever you wish.'

Rose forced a smile and insisted that she couldn't waste precious time in resting, but after some of the café's famous hot chocolate conceded that Dante's idea was a good one after all.

'Bene,' he said as they walked back to the hotel. 'Those beautiful eyes look heavy. We shall meet in the foyer at three, yes?'

She frowned. 'Look, Dante, I'm taking up a lot of your time. If you have other things to do—'

'What could be more important than spending time with you, Rose?'

'If you're sure—' A yawn overtook her mid-sentence, and Dante laughed.

'You see? A rest is good, yes?'

Rose nodded, embarrassed to feel glad of the rococo gilded cage instead of trudging up the stairs. 'If I stayed in Florence for any length of time I'd get very lazy.'

Dante smiled indulgently. 'It is good to be lazy sometimes, Rose. I shall see you at three—unless you would like to sleep longer than that?'

She shook her head. 'I'll be ready on the dot.'

Rose rang her mother for a brief update and

learned that Tom had collected Bea from nursery school, and afterwards the three of them had gone for a walk in the park to feed the ducks and buy ice cream.

'Did she cry for me in the night, Mum?'

'No, darling. She told me I wasn't quite as good at reading stories as Mummy, but otherwise settled down fairly well, and went off happy to school this morning. So do stop worrying. Enjoy yourself.'

Reassured, Rose had a brief rest on the bed, showered herself awake afterwards and changed the white tee for a navy polo shirt. When she saw Dante waiting for her in the foyer downstairs her unruly heart gave a thump as his eyes lit up at the sight of her. He was too good-looking by half, she thought resentfully as he took her hand.

'You slept, Rose?'

'I had a shower instead.'

'So did I.'

Since he was wearing a fresh shirt, his black curls were damp and he smelt delicious, Rose had already gathered that.

'Where now?' she asked as they left the hotel.

'To look at shops, *naturalmente*!'

Their first stop was on the Ponte Vecchio to look at the jewellery on display, but with her eyes popping at the prices Rose soon abandoned the jewellers for a shop selling silk ties.

'You want a gift for the boyfriend?' asked Dante.

Tempted to lie and say yes, she shook her head. 'For Tom, Charlotte's father.' She pointed to one in cream-dotted bronze silk. 'What do you think?'

'A good choice. What will you buy your mother?'

'I think I'll go for one of these silk scarves. Which do you fancy?'

Dante pointed to one in colours similar to the tie. 'That one, yes?'

Rose was very pleased with her purchases, sure she would have paid a lot more without Dante's help. Later, window-gazing at designer clothes in the Via da Tornabuoni, they spent fantastic pretend fortunes on a wardrobe for her before Dante took her to the Piazza della Repubblica to browse through La Rinascente, a department store where Rose could have spent hours.

'Next time stay longer and linger here as long as you wish. Also explore the Palazzo Pitti and the Tivoli Gardens,' Dante told her. 'But now, if you are not too tired, let us walk to Santa Croce to visit the Bar Vivoli Gelateria. The best ice cream in the world is made there.'

'An offer I can't resist!' She laughed up at him and saw his eyes light up. 'What?'

'At last you laugh! For a moment I saw the younger Rose again.'

The smile faded. 'A fleeting illusion, Dante.'

Their progress was slow on the way to the Vivoli due to the lure of the small shops in the Santa Croce area. In one of them Rose spotted attractive plaques in papier mâché painted with vegetables and bought a pair for her mother and Tom. 'They both love gardening, and these will be light enough to stow in my suitcase.'

He smiled. 'You have done much shopping for others, but nothing for yourself.'

'I don't need anything,' she assured him. She felt guilty enough about spending Fabio's money as it was. 'I'll settle for this ice cream you promised.'

At the Bar Vivoli Rose rolled her eyes in ecstasy when she tasted her strawberry ice cream. 'It's gorgeous—aren't you having any, Dante?'

He shook his head, smiling indulgently. 'I will protect the shopping from your gelato while you enjoy. Is there more you wish to buy? Or we could explore the great church of Santa Croce here.'

'I'd like to very much, but I'd better leave that for another time.' Not that there would be another time. She looked up at the magnificent facade with regret. 'Shall we go back now?'

'Whatever you wish, Rose. Where would you like to dine tonight?'

So he meant them to dine together again. Irritated by her pleasure at the prospect, she told him that at that moment, her palate still rocking with strawberry gelato, it was difficult to think of food. 'Maybe we could eat in the hotel again?' At least that way the cost of dinner would appear on her hotel bill and she would feel less obligated.

Dante frowned. 'If you really wish to. But there are many restaurants in Firenze. One of my favourites is right here in Santa Croce. We could take a taxi if you are tired. You can decide later when you have rested.'

She nodded. 'Fine.'

'I will see you at nine then, Rose.'

'I'll be ready. Are you taking a rest, too?'

He nodded. 'Also I must make a few phone calls, touch base, as you say. *Ciao.*'

Rose waited to make sure Dante stayed put in his room and then, praying she wouldn't get lost, hurried out of the hotel to make her way back to the Piazza della Repubblica to buy some of the delightful things she'd seen earlier in the department store. It might be Fabio's money, but he would approve of presents for Bea. When she got back she stowed her packages away in her suitcase and, feeling hot and grubby after her rushed, guilty shopping spree, checked her messages, grateful to find a brief but totally reassuring one from her mother. The other, at last, was from Charlotte, so obviously happy Rose felt a searing pang of envy for an instant before stepping into the shower, but afterwards fell into instant sleep so heavy it took the phone to wake her.

'Willow House Bookkeeping,' she muttered sleepily, and bit her lip at the sound of Dante's chuckle.

'You are in Firenze now, *cara*. You obviously slept well!'

She stifled a yawn. 'Very well.' She sat bolt upright after a look at her watch. 'And much too long!'

'*Bene*. You obviously needed this. Sleep longer if you wish.'

'No, indeed. Just give me half an hour and I'll be ready.'

'I shall knock on your door.'

Rose shot off the bed to wash and get to work on her face. Wishing she had something different to wear, she brushed her hair loose to ring the changes a little with the faithful black dress, and flung the scarf bought for her mother over one shoulder.

'You glow, *cara*,' Dante told her when she opened the door to him later.

'Surprising what a little nap can do for a girl.' She smiled guiltily. 'I thought Mum wouldn't mind if I wore her present just once first, but I must be careful not to get anything on it—no more gelato, for a start.'

'Should such a tragedy happen, I will buy you another. So, Rose, do you still wish to dine here, or would you like something more *animado*, where locals eat?'

'*Animado* with locals, definitely. And I'm perfectly happy to walk.' Maybe she could persuade him to let her go halves with the bill.

'Then I shall take you to a trattoria near the bar where you had your gelato. It is basic and traditional, and so popular it is always crowded.'

'Sounds good. Lead on.'

After her hot, furtive dash earlier on it was dangerously pleasant to stroll with Dante through the balmy warmth of the Florence evening. For one night like this she would pretend he was just a friend she was enjoying an evening with, rather than the man who'd once broken her heart and turned her life upside down. The trattoria was packed, as he had forecast, but a place was found for them in a long red-walled dining room filled with laughing, talking, gesticulating diners sitting elbow to elbow, in total contrast to the formality of the night before, and Rose loved it.

After discussion with the waiter who brought their menus Dante ordered wine and mineral water and sat back, amused to see Rose so obviously enjoying the proximity with her fellow diners.

'This is more like it,' she said with satisfaction, sneaking a look at the dishes set down at the next table. 'Will you help me choose, Dante?'

He leaned close to translate the names of the

dishes, and after much discussion about the various delights on offer Rose settled on a mixed grill of fish with spinach. 'I don't cook fish much at home, so this is a treat for me. What are you having?'

'I like your choice. I will have the same.' Dante nodded in approval as he studied the bottle of wine a waiter offered for his inspection. '*Grazie.* Try the wine, *cara*, and give me your opinion.'

'Mmm,' she said with relish. 'Gorgeous. What is it?'

'A Fortinari Classico,' he said with pride. 'I am impressed that they keep this range here.'

'Which means it's very pricey.' Rose drank a little more. 'I can see why.' She raised embarrassed eyes to his. 'I'm putting you to so much expense, Dante. Please let—'

'No!' he said flatly. 'To see you enjoy your dinner is reward enough.'

'I'm enjoying everything.' She looked round the packed, noisy dining room with pleasure. 'I love it here.' Her eyes sparkled as plates were set in front of them. '*Grazie,*' she said to the waiter.

Dante laughed indulgently as she sniffed in rapture. 'Enjoy, *carina.*'

'I will! It's a long time since that gelato.'

'So tell me about this house you live in,' Dante said later, after Rose had refused a *dolce* in favour of coffee.

'It's my own family home. Mum signed it over to me when she moved in with Tom. He wants them to get married,' she added, 'but Mum is happy the way things are, afraid that formalising the arrangement might change it. She believes in the saying "If it ain't broke don't fix it".'

Dante's eyes darkened. 'She is wise.'

Rose looked at him questioningly. 'Were you heartbroken when your wife left you?'

He gave a mirthless laugh. '*Dio*, no! My brother, as always, was right. I had a fortunate escape— forgive me, Rose. You cannot want to hear this.'

How wrong could a man be? 'Is Elsa still with the new man she left you for?'

'Yes, though *new* is not the right word.' Dante's expressive mouth turned down. 'Enrico Calvi is old enough to be her father, but so wealthy Elsa is now enjoying a life of idle luxury.'

'She wanted to do that?'

'Oh, yes.' He smiled sardonically. 'Younger faces—and bodies—were winning the top jobs.

She was glad to abandon her career while still known as a supermodel. *Allora*, I no longer see her face on magazine covers everywhere to remind me of my folly.'

'Is she very beautiful still?'

He nodded carelessly. 'I have not seen her since she left, but Elsa was obsessed with her looks and I doubt she has changed much. Calvi has children from a former marriage and does not demand the babies that would ruin his trophy wife's perfect body. I, fool that I was, wanted children very much.'

Rose drank some water, suddenly sorry she'd eaten so much as her stomach lurched at Dante's heartfelt admission.

His mouth tightened. 'She waited until our wedding night to tell me she had no intention of having babies. Ever. But no more talk of Elsa.' Dante looked at Rose in silence for a while, his blue eyes intent. 'Now I must take you back. I wish you could stay longer, Rose.'

'Not possible, I'm afraid.'

'*Que peccato*! In the morning I will drive you to the airport in Pisa—unless you would prefer the train journey?' He beckoned to a waiter to bring the bill.

'No, indeed. But won't that take up too much of your time?'

'It is not far out of my way home,' he assured her, 'and will give me the pleasure of more time with you before you leave. But this will not be goodbye, Rose. I shall see you when I come to England again next.'

Her heart lurched. If Dante still wanted babies no way was she letting him anywhere near Bea. He took her arm to steer her past an approaching entwined couple as they walked back, the contact raising her pulse rate even higher.

Rose paused when they reached the foot of the hotel steps, her eyes raised to the handsome, intent face. 'This has been a lovely evening, Dante. Not the kind of thing that features much in my life as a rule.'

'Yet Charlotte told me you have someone in your life.'

'He's a friend from my college days.'

'But surely you will marry one day, Rose?'

She shrugged. 'I doubt it.'

Dante held the door open for her. 'When you see

Charlotte so happy with Fabio, do you not wish for a relationship like theirs?' His eyes darkened as they made for the lift. 'I have always envied them their marriage.'

'They're very lucky.'

Dante halted when they reached her room. '*Ascolta*, it is early yet, Rose. I would so much like to sit with you on your balcony and talk for a while longer like old friends. I can order tea. You would like that?'

She looked at him in silence for a moment. 'All right, Dante.' She gave him a wry smile. 'But only because you said the magic word.'

His smile mirrored hers. 'Friends?'

'No—tea!'

Dante laughed and rang room service. After a waiter arrived with a tray Dante tipped him and closed the door behind him then pulled up two of the chairs to the metal table on the balcony overlooking the moonlit Arno. Rose poured tea and the coffee Dante had ordered for himself, and sat back in her chair, eyeing him warily.

'So what shall we talk about?'

'You, Rose. Tell me why you started your own business.'

'I applied for accountancy jobs but didn't get the ones I wanted, so I decided to use my training for something else and eventually hit on bookkeeping.'

'Ah,' said Dante, nodding. 'You went to college again for this?'

'No. I did an eighteen-month home study course accredited by the Institute of Certified Bookkeepers, and managed to complete it in just over three months.' Rose drained her cup and refilled it. 'My mother was a huge help. So was Tom. He found a web designer for me and made sure I informed HM Revenue and Customs, and took out indemnity insurance to cover me while working in clients' offices. I also got a practising licence...' She paused, biting her lip. 'This is probably boring you rigid, Dante.'

He shook his head decisively. 'I am enthralled. You were so young to achieve all this, Rose. I am impressed.'

'I had a lot of things going for me,' she reminded him. 'With such wonderful support from my mother and Tom, a home of my own with a room I can use for an office—and with my brain still in gear from my finals—I managed to get the new qualification quickly. I now divide my time between working at home and in travelling to small businesses grateful enough for my help and my reasonable charges to pass on my name to new clients.'

'You make a good living from this?'

'It was a slow start, but I've now done well enough to pay back the money my mother lent me for the original expenses for certification and optional exams and the web design and so on.' Rose took a look at the clear-cut profile outlined by the light from her room. 'So now you know all about me, Dante.'

He shook his head. 'I think not. One day I hope to learn much, much more—but not tonight. I will leave you now to your sleep.' He raised her hand to his lips. '*Buonanotte*. I shall see you in the morning. Since we must leave early, you would like breakfast brought to your room?'

Rose nodded. 'Will you order it for me, please?'

'*Subito*. And in the morning I shall ring you when it is time to leave.' He went to the door and turned to smile at her. 'Now lock it, *per favore*.'

Rose spent a restless night after the conversation with Dante. His talk of babies terrified her. If he found out that Bea was his child what would he do? What would she do, if it came to that? She eventually lapsed into a restless doze but woke early, and after a horrified look in the mirror stood under a hot shower until she felt, and looked, more human. By the time her breakfast arrived her hair was dry and she was dressed for travelling, her bags packed.

Soon afterwards, Dante rang. '*Buongiorno, Rose.*'

'Good morning. I'm ready. I just have to sort the bill.'

'I will be with you in one second.'

When Rose opened her door Dante smiled at her denim jeans and casual jacket. 'You look so young, like a student again.' He took her suitcase. 'I will put this in the car, which is waiting outside. Forgive me if I stay there with it until you are ready to leave.'

'Of course. I'll join you as quickly as I can.' Armed with her credit card, Rose approached the suave receptionist to ask for her bill.

'All was settled in advance; there is nothing to pay.' He handed her a receipted bill. 'Signor Fortinari waits outside in the car,' he added. 'I trust you enjoyed your stay?'

She smiled. 'I did. Very much. Goodbye and thank you.'

'*Arrivederci* and safe journey, Miss Palmer.'

Rose felt uneasy as she left the hotel, wondering if she should have asked for an itemised version of the bill for Fabio, but forgot her worries when she saw the car waiting at the foot of the steps. It was sleek and scarlet and as handsome as the man who jumped out of the driver's seat as she approached.

'Wow, Dante, great car!'

He laughed as he handed her inside. 'This is my one indulgence—she's a sports car but also practical. She has four doors, also four-wheel drive, which is of much use to me in some parts of the country. You like her?'

'What's not to like? She's obviously the love of your life.'

'*Davvero*—see how she responds to me?'

Rose laughed and sank back in the seat, feeling the power vibrate through her body when Dante switched on the ignition. 'What more can a man ask?'

He shot her a sidelong glance as he drove away from the hotel. 'Those things a machine cannot do for a man.'

Annoyed to feel her face flush, Rose made no response as she settled down to enjoy the drive, content just to look at the passing landscape as they left the city. She relaxed as she breathed in the aroma of expensive new car, and whatever Dante had used in the shower. 'This is a big improvement on the train journey,' she commented when they were speeding along the *autostrada*. 'I tried to look at the scenery I was passing through on the way here in the train, but I couldn't concentrate.'

'Why not?'

'I was tired after all the effort it took to juggle appointments and so on before getting away.' Plus her worries that Bea might be unhappy without her, and the strain of wondering what was wrong with Charlotte.

'If your mother is looking after your business while you are away she will be pleased to see you back, Rose.'

'Unless she's cross with me for buying presents.'

Dante laughed. 'If so, you may blame me for

encouraging your extravagance. But you are very close to your mother, yes?'

Rose nodded, smiling. 'But we have clashes of temperament sometimes.'

'My mother had many with my sister Mirella in the past, but now she is Nonna to several grand-children the clashes happen only when she spoils them too much.'

'How many nieces and nephews do you have?'

'Five. Mirella and Franco have two sons and a daughter, and Leo and Harriet one of each.'

'Harriet?'

Dante nodded. 'My brother's wife is English. You would like her.'

Rose was intrigued. 'How did they meet?'

'It is such a strange story I shall leave it until next time I see you. I must concentrate now as the traffic is heavy.'

Dante insisted on waiting at Galileo Galilei Air-port with Rose until she was ready to board the plane, and took note of her telephone numbers and her address while passengers surged around them as constant announcements filled the air. 'I will be in London next month to meet an old friend of mine, Luke Armytage,' he told her. 'He is a master of wine and owner of a chain of wine stores which retail our best vintages. I shall come to see you then, Rose, but I will consult you first to make sure you are free.'

'Goodbye then, Dante.' Rose smiled at him brightly as her flight was called. 'And thank you yet again.'

'Prego.' Without warning, he seized her in his arms and kissed her full on the mouth. He raised his head to stare down into her startled eyes and then kissed her again at such length they were both breathless when he released her. *'Arrivederci,* Rose.'

Afraid to trust her voice, she managed a shaky smile and hurried away after the other passengers.

Dante stood watching as his heartbeat slowed, his smile wry when it became obvious that Rose had no intention of looking back.

The flight home was tiring. Rose spent most of it convincing herself that there was no danger of falling in love with Dante Fortinari again, even after the electrifying effect of his goodbye kiss, which, from the look on his face, had affected Dante in pretty much the same way. She was human and female enough to find this deeply gratifying, but she would make sure it never happened again. No way could she let him back into her life. She would have to tell him about Bea, and then she would be forced to tell her mother the truth at last, that Dante Fortinari was her child's father. And then Tom would know, and so would Charlotte, and Fabio, and everyone else involved once she started the ball rolling. By the time Rose boarded the Pennington coach at Birmingham Airport, she had decided against any such dramatic upheaval in her tidy little life. If Dante did ring to ask to see her again she would take the coward's way out and refuse to see him.

CHAPTER THREE

WHEN THE CAB stopped outside Willow House the front door flew open while Rose was paying the driver, and a little girl dressed in jeans and T-shirt hurtled down the garden path with the tall figure of Tom Morley in hot pursuit. Rose abandoned her suitcase and swept her child up in her arms, kissing her all over her rosy, indignant face.

'Where you *been*, Mummy?' demanded Bea, struggling to get down. 'You didn't sleep in your bed for lots of nights!'

'Only *two* nights, darling. Have you been a good girl?'

Beatrice Grace Palmer nodded happily. 'Lots of times.' She tugged on her mother's hand. 'Come *on*. Me and Gramma did baking.'

'The cakes smell delicious, too,' said Tom, taking charge of the suitcase. He kissed Rose's cheek. 'You look tired, pet.'

'Only from travelling.' Rose smiled as Grace

Palmer appeared in the doorway, looking too youthful in jeans and jersey to be anyone's grandmother. 'Talking of tired, how's Gramma?'

Grace hugged her daughter. 'I'm just fine.' She grinned triumphantly at Tom. 'We coped very well, if I do say so myself.'

Rose allowed herself to be towed straight to the kitchen, where little iced cakes sat on a wire tray. 'Look, Mummy,' said Bea, bouncing in her little pink sneakers. 'Fairy cakes!'

'They look gorgeous. Let's have them for pudding after our lunch, which is something delicious from the yummy smell coming from the oven.'

'Nothing fancy, darling,' said Grace. 'I offered several menu suggestions to celebrate your return from foreign parts, but cottage pie won the majority vote. So come on, Bea. Let's put the cakes away in the tin so we can lay the table, and we all need to wash before we eat.'

'Bea and I will lay the table,' said Tom, 'and let Mummy wash first.'

'Hurry *up*, Mummy,' ordered Bea. 'I'm hungry.'

'I need another kiss,' said Rose huskily, and picked her daughter up to hug her.

Bea obliged her with a smacking kiss. 'I cried for you last night, so Gramma cuddled me.'

Rose blinked hard. 'Then you were a lucky girl. Gramma's the best at cuddling.'

Tom nodded in vigorous agreement over the curly fair head, winning a flushed, sparkling look from Grace as he took Bea from her mother. 'Come on, Honey Bea. Let's wash those paws.'

Rose hurried upstairs to her room and took a depressed look in the mirror as she hung up her clothes. Far from benefiting from her little holiday, she looked as weary and wan as she felt.

Lunch was a lively affair with much input from Bea about her activities in her mother's absence. 'I went to school *all* day yesterday, then to the park with Gramma and Tom.'

'I bet they enjoyed that!' said Rose, grinning.

'We did,' agreed Grace, and relieved her granddaughter of her plate. 'What a star—you ate the vegetables, too. You liked that, darling?'

'Yummy!' said Bea, and gave Rose a smile exactly like her father's. 'Cake now?'

Rose waited expectantly, eyebrows raised.

'Please!' Bea beamed in triumph.

'Good girl.'

After cakes had been devoured, Rose said casually, 'I'd better find some things I bought in Florence.'

'Where's that?' demanded Bea.

'It's a town near where Auntie Charlotte lives in Italy. I had to fly there on a plane. You can help me carry the parcels.'

Later that evening, after a rapturous Bea had tried on her new jeans and T-shirts, and the exquisite little dress that Rose hadn't been able to resist, the child was finally tucked up in bed with her new cuddly Pinocchio before Rose could finally relax over supper with her mother and Tom and give details of her trip. She told Charlotte's tale with care, not sure how much she was supposed to divulge to Tom.

'Good God!' He eyed Rose in disbelief as she finished. 'Charlotte finally got you there, only to take off somewhere else?'

Grace put a hand on his arm. 'No harm done, love. Rose had her first real break since Bea was born, and hopefully she was able to enjoy it, knowing that her baby girl was safe with us.'

He frowned. 'But the fact remains that Charlotte stranded Rose alone in a strange country while she went swanning off to New York with Fabio. How did you manage, pet?'

Rose braced herself. 'Charlotte asked Dante Fortinari to deliver a letter to the hotel to brief me. You remember him from the wedding, Tom?'

'Of course I do. Charming fellow—got married shortly after Charlotte.'

'But his wife left him pretty quickly, stupid woman,' said Grace, eyeing her daughter. 'You got on with him very well at the wedding, I seem to remember.'

Rose nodded. 'He was great fun.'

Tom shook his head in disapproval. 'I shall have words with my daughter next time she rings. Now, tell me why she was so determined to get you to Florence. Lord knows she's asked you often enough before, so what made this occasion so different?'

'Tom,' said Grace gently, 'perhaps Rose thinks Charlotte should tell you that.'

Rose sighed. 'I do, but on the other hand, Tom, if it's going to worry you it's pointless to keep you in the dark.' She recounted Charlotte's suspicions about Fabio, followed by her remorse afterwards when she discovered the truth. 'Fabio insisted I should stay at the hotel anyway, all expenses paid.'

Grace shook her head in wonder. 'How on earth could Charlotte suspect Fabio of straying? The man adores her!'

'And spoils her far more than I ever did,' said Tom and raised an eyebrow at Rose. 'So where does Fortinari come into this?'

'He volunteered to show me round Florence.' Rose smiled brightly. 'Which was kind. I would have been a bit lost on my own.'

'I should damn well think you would.' Tom got up to hold out his hand to Grace. 'Come on, love, we must let this girl get to bed. She looks done in.'

'I could stay, if you like, Rose, and get up with Bea if she's wakeful tonight?' her mother offered.

'Absolutely not,' said Rose, laughing. 'You've done more than enough, both of you. Though I'm afraid I'll need you tomorrow afternoon for a couple of hours, Mum, if you can? A client got in touch while I was away so I'm driving to see her.'

'Of course.' Grace kissed her daughter goodnight, and thanked her again for the presents. 'You shouldn't have been so extravagant.'

Rose smiled. 'Dante got a far better price for

them than I would have done, and in any case it was Fabio's money.'

'Then we'll both enjoy our booty free of guilt,' said Tom, eyes twinkling.

Later Rose checked on her sleeping child, longing to kiss the rosy cheek but too tired to risk waking her up. Yawning, she went next door to her own room, glad to crawl into bed. It had been an odd sort of holiday. The stay in Florence had been too short, the air travel too tiring and her taste of the *dolce vita* with Dante too unsettling. It would take effort to knuckle down to routine again. Not that she had a choice. And though most people, like Dante, thought her job boring, her travels to meet with clients made it far less so than being confined to an office all day. As she reached to turn out the light her phone rang.

'Rose?' said a husky, unmistakable voice.

She sat bolt upright. 'Dante!'

'Did all go well on your journey?'

'It did, and now I'm back where I belong.'

'I do not agree with that,' he said, surprising her. 'In Firenze you belonged there. I shall be in London soon and will drive to see you.'

Rose was about to veto the idea when Dante went on without pausing.

'Now I know you are safe I will let you sleep. *Buonanotte*, Rose.'

'Good night. Thanks for ringing,' she said politely.

His chuckle sent tremors down her spine. 'You knew that I would. *Ciao.*'

Rose switched off the light and slid down in the bed, but thanks to Dante's call she was no longer tired. The mere sound of his voice had conjured up not only his goodbye kiss but all her doubts and fears about keeping his daughter secret from him. But he had no legal right to claim Bea as his daughter, she reassured herself with a resurgence of the old resentment. His sole contribution to her existence was a fleeting episode of sexual pleasure before he'd returned to the fiancée he'd neglected to mention.

When Bea had been dropped off at nursery school the next morning Rose got down to work right away to make up for lost time. Usually she did some household chores before settling at her desk, but Grace had left the house in remarkably immaculate condition for someone in charge of a lively child. Rose sighed. In the beginning, after Bea was born, she had tried hard to transform herself from slapdash student into perfect mother, housekeeper and eventual wage earner. She'd learned the hard way to get her priorities right. As long as Bea was happy, clean and well fed Rose took her mother's advice and kept her brief spells of spare time for taking the baby for walks, or resting while Bea napped. The chores could wait until Rose had time and energy to spare for them. Or, said Grace, she could accept money to pay for a little help in the house.

Rose switched on her computer, smiling at the memory of her indignation at the suggestion. She'd been so determined to be the most efficient single parent it was possible to be. And if she was sometimes desperate for a good night's sleep, or to be out clubbing or shopping with girl-friends again, or even just taking a walk without pushing a buggy, she never admitted it to a soul. She sighed irritably and settled down to work in the brief window of time before she collected her daughter.

Bea's face lit up when she saw her mother waiting for her. 'Mummy! You came today.'

'Of course I did.' Rose took her leave of the young teacher and held Bea's hand. 'I told you I would.'

'You didn't come yesterday.'

'I was away, so I asked Gramma and Tom to fetch you.'

Bea nodded as she was buckled into her car seat. 'They fetched me lots of times.'

'Only two times, darling.'

Bea looked unconvinced by the maths. 'Are you going to work today?'

'Yes, but only for a little while this afternoon. Gramma will stay with you and I'll be home in time for tea. And tomorrow it's Saturday and we can go to the park.'

Rose was soon so firmly entrenched in her usual routine again it was hard to believe the trip to Florence had ever happened until Charlotte rang to grovel with apologies and demand every detail of Rose's taste of *la dolce vita*.

Rose brushed that aside. 'Did you ask Dante Fortinari to show me round, Charlotte?'

'Certainly not. I just asked him to deliver your letter by hand because there was cash in it.' Charlotte paused. 'Though Dante seemed pretty keen on meeting up with you again.'

'He was very kind,' said Rose colourlessly. 'And,' she added with more bite, 'I would have been a bit lost in Florence if he hadn't turned up.'

'I know, I know,' said Charlotte remorsefully. 'But if Dante looked after you it all worked out in the end.'

'As did your problem,' Rose pointed out. 'You were mad to think Fabio would cheat on you!'

'Hormonal, not mad.' Charlotte drew in an audible breath. 'I behaved like a total idiot because— wait for the roll of drums—I'm pregnant at last.'

Rose gave a screech of delight. 'Oh, Charlotte, how *wonderful*. I'm so happy for you. Have you told your father?'

'No. I'll ring him right away now I've told you. I waited until I was absolutely sure before spreading the glad news. I didn't even tell Fabio until we were in New York.'

'But surely he was wondering?'

'Of course he was, but I've been late before so he was afraid to say a word, especially because I'd been a bit standoffish with him due to my crazy suspicions. But now I'm so happy I don't even mind the morning sickness part—at least not too much.' Charlotte came to a halt. 'So, Rose, are you still mad at me?'

'For giving me a luxury, all-expenses-paid holiday in one of the most beautiful cities in the world? No, Signora Vilari, I'm not. Now, hurry up and ring Tom so I can share the glad news with Mum.'

Once the excitement about Charlotte's news had died down Rose was soon back in her usual dual role of mother and businesswoman, until Dante rang one morning to say he would be with her the next day to take her out to dinner. She stiffened her resolve and told him that she was working and wouldn't be available.

'Is this true, Rose, or do you mean you have no wish to see me?'

She sighed. 'All right, I'm not working, but I think it's best we don't see each other again.'

There was silence on the line for a moment. 'I frightened you with my kiss?'

'Of course not. The thing is, Dante, I'm grateful

for the time you took to show me round Florence, but it was just a one-off kind of thing.'

'You are refusing to see me any more?' he demanded, his voice hard.

'Yes. I am. You live in Italy and I live here, so it would be pointless, anyway.'

'*Allora*, you have not forgiven me.'

'For what, exactly?' she snapped.

'For making love to you and then leaving you so suddenly that night.'

'Oh, that. No forgiveness necessary. These things happen.'

'If not that, then I demand to know what is wrong, Rose.'

'Do you, indeed! Goodbye, Dante.' Rose switched off her phone and slumped down on the sofa, determined not to cry. She'd done enough crying over Dante Fortinari in the past. But no matter how hard she tried to control them, the tears came pouring down her face just the same and she had to do some hasty face scrubbing in case Bea saw Mummy crying.

Grace popped in later for coffee and frowned when she saw Rose's swollen eyes. 'Darling, what's wrong?'

'Dante rang. He wanted to take me out to dinner tomorrow.'

'But that's good, surely, not something to cry about?'

Rose sniffed inelegantly. 'I turned him down.'

Grace stared at her blankly. 'Why?' Her eyes narrowed suddenly. 'This is about Bea, isn't it?'

'What...what do you mean?'

'You don't want him to know about her. Bea's not a dark secret, darling—it's time you got that idea out of your system.'

Rose's heart settled back into place again. 'You're right. Lord knows, my situation is hardly unusual. I saw the percentages of single parent families in the headlines on my computer only this morning.'

'And, as one of them, you do brilliantly, darling.'

'Ah, but I wouldn't be without help from you and Tom. And,' Rose added with sudden passion, 'don't ever think I forget that, not for a minute.'

'I don't. So why not ring Dante back and say you've changed your mind? We'll have Bea for a sleepover and keep her out of the way if that would make things easier for you?'

Rose shook her head obstinately. 'I'm not going to see him again.'

'Why not? How often will you have a date with someone like Dante Fortinari?' Grace gave a wicked grin as she straightened. 'Your old pal Stuart Porter is very nice, but gorgeous and Italian he isn't.'

Rose laughed ruefully. Her mother had hit the nail on the head. Quite apart from Dante as escort, expensive dinners were not part of her social life. A night out with Stuart meant a trip to the cinema and sometimes coffee or a drink afterwards, all of which she enjoyed occasionally. But dinner with Dante would have been in a different league.

'Look, darling, why don't we have Bea for a sleepover tomorrow anyway, and you have a whole evening to yourself and a good night's sleep afterwards? You look as though you could do with it.'

'I know that.' Rose eyed her mother doubtfully. 'I love my daughter, but a night to myself does sound tempting.'

'Right. We'll come for her about four. She can eat with us as a special treat and we'll take her to school next morning, too, so you can make the most of *your* special treat.'

Bea was wildly excited the next day when she learned about the sleepover with Gramma and Tom. She loved the bedroom they had created for her there, so useful if Rose was ever travelling away overnight for work.

'Are you going out with Stuart?' asked Bea suspiciously as they packed her shiny pink holdall.

'No, not tonight. Why? Don't you like him?' On the odd occasions that she'd run into Stuart while out with Bea his embarrassment had been so plain her bright little daughter had picked up on it.

Bea shook her curly head in disdain. 'He calls me little girl.'

'Ah. His mistake, because you're a *big* girl! Shall I put Pinocchio in here with Bear or will you carry him?'

'Carry him.' Bea hugged the toy to her chest possessively, and then beamed as the doorbell rang. 'Gramma! Can I open the door?'

'Go down slowly,' called Rose. She collected a couple of books and followed with the bag, suddenly aware that it was very quiet below instead of Bea's usual joyful reunion with Grace. She flew down to the hall to find her daughter scowling at the man smiling down at her.

'*Buonasera*, Rose,' said Dante. 'Will you introduce me to this beautiful young lady?'

Struck dumb for a moment, Rose's first reaction was fury because all her cloak and dagger efforts had been useless. Dante was face to face with her child and, as a second strike against him, Mummy looked a mess while he, as always, looked wonderful. 'Why are you here?' she demanded.

His smile faded. 'I hope to change your mind about dining with me. But I make a mistake, yes?'

Dante's English was usually so good it was obvious she'd thrown him off balance.

'Not at all,' said Rose coolly. 'Do come in.'

Bea clutched Pinocchio to her chest, glaring balefully at the visitor.

'My name is Dante Fortinari,' he told her. 'What is yours, *bella*?'

'Beatrice Grace Palmer,' she announced militantly.

'My daughter,' said Rose, in case he was in any doubt.

'You are very fortunate,' said Dante, looking up

from the fair curls to meet Rose's eyes. 'Perhaps we could dine early and take Beatrice with us?'

'No!' wailed Bea, incensed. 'I want to go to Gramma's.'

To Rose's relief, the doorbell rang again. 'Go and open the door again then, darling. This time it *is* Gramma; Tom, too, I expect.'

'Mrs Palmer, Mr Morley, I am delighted to see you again,' said Dante, shaking hands with the surprised pair in turn as they exchanged greetings. He smiled wryly. 'I came with hope to change Rose's mind about dining with me.'

'I'm sure she'd be delighted to do that,' said Grace, narrowing her eyes at her daughter as Bea swarmed up into Tom's arms and sat there, secure and hostile, scowling at Dante.

'Are you packed and ready, Honey Bea?' asked Tom. 'If so, we'll take you home to supper.'

'Yes, come along, darling,' said Grace, manfully ignoring the undercurrents simmering in the hall of Willow House. 'It was lovely to meet you again, Dante.'

'My pleasure, *signora*.' He smiled at the little girl in Tom's arms. 'It was a pleasure to meet you, too, *bella*.'

Another scowl was the only response.

'Bea,' said Rose in a tone the child knew well.

'Sorry,' she said and then, to everyone's surprise, gave Dante her most irresistible smile. 'Not Bella. I'm Bea.'

He returned the smile in delight. 'I apologise!'

'Bye-bye,' she said firmly, hugging Pinocchio closer.

'Be a good girl for Gramma and Tom,' Rose reminded her.

'She always is,' said Tom, bending the truth a little.

Rose waved as the trio went down the garden path then closed the door and turned to face her visitor.

'Why did you not tell me you had a daughter?' Dante demanded before she could say a word.

Rose's chin lifted. 'If you're inferring that I'm in any way ashamed of her, I assure you I'm not!'

He held up a hand. *'Pace, pace.* How could you be ashamed of such a beautiful child? Yet if I had not ignored your refusal to see me I would not have met her. You did not want me to?'

'No, I didn't.'

His eyes narrowed. 'Because her father objects?'

'No, nothing like that.' Rose sighed 'Oh, well, now you're here, come into the kitchen. I'll make coffee.'

Dante shrugged off his suede jacket as he followed her. *'Permesso?'*

'Of course. Do sit down.'

He took a chair at the table, his eyes on the artwork adorning the walls. 'These are by Beatrice?'

Rose nodded. 'Yes. As you can see, she's heavily into red and orange. And, as she informed you, we call her Bea.' She made coffee, then laid a tray and brought it all over to the table. 'Would you like something to eat?'

'Nothing, *grazie.*' Dante's eyes met hers. 'You are angry with me for intruding, Rose?'

'Only because I would have preferred to tell you about Bea before you met her.'

'But since you refused to see me again, when would you have done that?' he demanded, looking down his nose with hauteur. 'You are obviously uneasy because I have come here against your wish. Is there a jealous lover or, worse, a husband, who would object to my presence here?'

'Neither.' She sat down wearily. 'I suppose you may as well know the truth. Bea is the result of a one-night stand with someone who has no idea he's a father. I'm not ashamed of my child, only of the circumstances that brought her into the world.'

Dante sat down abruptly, colour draining from his olive skin. He leaned forward and grasped her hand. 'You were—forced, *cara*?'

'No, nothing like that! I just drank one glass of wine too many one night to celebrate my results.'

'And you did not tell this man what happened?'

'No.' Rose felt her face heat. 'At the time I was working as a waitress while I applied for jobs, and put my lack of energy—and other things—down to being on my feet so much. It was a couple of months before it even dawned on me that I could be pregnant.'

Dante's grasp tightened. 'What happened then?'

Rose drew in a deep, unsteady breath. 'I told my mother and gave her the glad news that I had no intention of contacting the father. Tom, of course, was ready to hunt him down and force him to take responsibility. Fabio and Charlotte too.'

'Naturalmente,' said Dante harshly. 'Did they find him?'

'No. I refused to give his name.'

'*Dio!*' He raked a hand through his hair. 'Your mother found this hard, yes?'

Rose nodded. 'So did Charlotte. But she was hugely supportive, flew over to see me a lot during the pregnancy and even insisted on being present at the actual birth.'

'She is a good friend,' said Dante, nodding. 'She was very unhappy about deserting you in Firenze, Rose.'

'Is that why you volunteered to look after me?'

'No. I was most delighted to do so.' He eyed her narrowly. 'I so much enjoyed our brief time together there, but you think it is a mistake to meet again, yes?'

'I'm sorry I was so rude, but finding you talking to my daughter was a shock.' She sighed. 'When I first found out I was pregnant I was in such a state I begged Charlotte and Fabio to keep it secret from the wedding guests I'd met because there's no father in the picture.'

'Yet there is one somewhere who has no idea he has a daughter.' Dante shook his head. 'Having met your child, I feel sympathy for him.'

'Too late to tell him now; he'd never believe me,' said Rose flatly.

Dante looked at her in silence for a moment, his eyes intent on hers. 'You are going out tonight?'

'No.'

'Yet your child has gone to stay overnight with your mother and Signor Morley, yes?'

'Yes.' Rose coloured. 'Mum thought I could do with some time to myself.'

'So what will you do? Read, watch television?'

'Probably.'

'While I go back to my hotel for a lonely dinner.' He reached across the table and took her hand. 'Change your mind. Dine with me, Rose.'

Now he was here, with the touch of his hand sending heat rushing through her, Rose found it hard to imagine why she'd ever said no to him in the first place. 'All right.' She ignored the warning bells going off in her head. 'But you'll have to wait while I made myself more presentable.'

His smile took her breath away. '*Bene*! I will go back to the hotel to make myself more presentable also and return for you later.'

'Thank you,' said Rose, wondering if she'd made a huge mistake. At least her mother and Tom would be pleased. They worried about her lack of social life.

'And this time I will be more welcome, yes?'

Her eyes softened. 'Sorry I was so hostile, Dante.'

'Non importa,' he assured her, and smiled as he collected his jacket. 'Your daughter was even more hostile, no?'

'It was a new experience for her.'

'The friends who take you out do not call for you here?'

'No. I meet them in town.'

Dante nodded. 'And drive yourself home afterwards so you can leave when you wish?'

'Exactly.'

'I shall return at seven-thirty—and not a minute sooner. *D'accordo*?'

Rose nodded. 'I'll be ready.' She opened her front door and smiled when she saw the sleek hire car. 'Nice wheels again, Dante.'

'Not as nice as my own, though,' he said with regret and returned the smile, his eyes warm again. 'I look forward to our evening, Rose. *Ciao.*'

'Ciao,' she echoed as he drove off, and shook her head. Her efforts to keep her life private had been a total waste of time.

Rose hurried upstairs to shower and give herself

a makeover. She couldn't compete with Dante's faithless Elsa, but she could look pretty good when she made the effort. When she was ready she eyed her reflection critically and took heart in the fact that even in the clinging caramel jersey of her Christmas present dress her baby bulge was hardly noticeable now, due to constant boring exercises.

She went downstairs, wondering why she was doing this. After the delight Dante had taken in Bea earlier, she should have sent him packing right then to avoid any future danger. But she'd silenced her head and given in to the heart which urged her to make the most of an opportunity that would probably never happen again.

When she opened the door to Dante later the heated look he gave her was worth all her hard work. 'Rose, you are ravishing!'

'Thank you, kind sir. You look pretty good yourself. Nice threads.'

'*Cosa?*'

'Great suit.'

'*Grazie.* I like your dress also.'

'Thank you.'

Rose had expected Dante to treat her to dinner at the Chesterton, the best hotel in town, but she stiffened as she realised he was driving out into the country to a venue they eventually approached down a long tree-lined drive. The Hermitage was so well-known for luxurious comfort combined with the warmth of a family-owned hotel that Charlotte had chosen it for her wedding.

Before Rose could ask why Dante had brought her there, a large, vaguely familiar man came out to greet them, hand outstretched to clap Dante on the shoulder.

'Introduce me, then.'

'This lovely lady is Miss Rose Palmer, Tony.' Dante turned to Rose. 'Rose, allow me to present my cousin, Anthony Mostyn, owner of the Hermitage—also of the Chesterton in town.'

Rose smiled as Tony Mostyn shook her hand. 'How do you do?'

'A pleasure to meet you, Miss Palmer. A shame my wife's taken the children to her mother's for a couple of days. We could have made a foursome for dinner.'

'Give Allegra a kiss from me and tell her we look forward to seeing her next time. What is good on the menu tonight, Tony?' asked Dante.

'Everything,' said Tony promptly, 'including your usual choice. So enjoy the meal. I'll catch up with you later.'

'What is wrong, Rose?' asked Dante when they were seated in the bar.

'This is where we met at Charlotte's wedding,' she said tonelessly, and looked him in the eye. 'I remember seeing Tony Mostyn at the time, and thinking he looked young to run the Hermitage. You didn't tell me you were related.'

'It is not the dark secret. My aunt, Anna Fortinari, married Huw Mostyn, Tony's father, but tragically they were killed in an air crash a few years ago. Tony is now managing director of the company that runs both hotels. His sister used to work in the business with him, but she married a Frenchman and lives in Paris now.' Dante surveyed the crowd in the bar. 'Tony does well.' His eyes were sombre as he turned back to her. 'I thought you would like to come here again, Rose, to the place where we first met. But this is another mistake, yes?'

'Yes,' she said bluntly, her eyes narrowing as a waiter arrived with a bottle of champagne.

'Mr Mostyn's compliments, sir,' he said, and filled their glasses.

Dante told him to convey their thanks and turned to Rose with a frown. 'Why did you look at me so?'

'I thought you were reminding me that I drank too much champagne last time I was here.'

His mouth tightened. '*Dio*, you find it very easy to think badly of me. For which you have good reason.' He lifted a shoulder, his eyes taking on the cold, hard look she'd seen before. The silence lengthened between them. 'This evening is a bad idea, yes?' he said at last.

'No.' Rose felt sudden remorse. 'It's lovely here, Dante, and a great treat for me.' Oh, God, that sounded so pathetic. 'But if you prefer to drive me home right now I wouldn't blame you. I've been utterly petty and graceless—'

'Because I brought you here, where we first met?' Dante moved closer. 'I hoped it would bring back pleasant memories. But perhaps all you remember is the way I left you so suddenly—'

'And then went on to marry the fiancée you forgot to mention to me.' To her angry dismay, her eyes filled with tears.

'For which I felt great guilt afterwards.' Dante gave her a pristine white handkerchief and then filled their glasses. 'Do not cry, *bella*. We must drink some of this champagne or Tony will ask questions.'

Rose dabbed at her eyes, thankful they were seated in a corner where no one would notice. She managed a smile and picked up her glass. 'Has my mascara run?'

Dante checked them out. 'No, Rose. Those beautiful dark eyes are still perfect.'

She raised her glass. 'What shall we drink to?'

'To more evenings together like this, but without the tears!' Dante drained his glass and signalled to a waiter that they were ready to order.

'You know, Dante,' said Rose, thinking about it, 'I've eaten more meals with you recently than with anyone other than Bea.'

'That pleases me very much.' He smiled at her over one of the huge menus. 'What would you like tonight? I always choose roast beef with the Yorkshire pudding when I am here.' He laughed as she looked at him in astonishment. *'Davvero!'*

Now she'd recovered from their disturbing little exchange Rose found her appetite had recovered with it. 'Actually, that sounds really good. Make it two.'

Dante gave the order to the waiter then sat back. 'Perhaps next time we can take your little Bea out for a meal. Would she like that?'

'She would.' Though Rose had no intention of letting it happen.

He smiled and refilled her glass. 'I also. I often take my nephews and nieces out, though not all of them at once! You must bring little Bea to meet them next time you come.'

Rose sighed. 'That won't be any time soon.'

'Because of your work?'

'Partly, yes.'

He eyed her questioningly. 'If the expense is also a problem I would be happy—'

'Certainly not!' she said, so sharply people nearby looked round. 'Sorry,' muttered Rose, crimsoning. 'But I can't take money from you, Dante. I feel beholden enough already because you paid for so much in Florence.'

'Is it so hard to accept things from me?' he demanded in a fierce undertone. 'I ask for nothing in return, if that is your fear.'

'I know that.' She bit her lip. 'The thing is,

Dante, ever since Bea was born I've tried very hard to live on what I earn from my business. I refuse hand outs, even from my mother. Though she paid for what I'm wearing today by calling it a Christmas present.'

'She is a clever lady.' Dante relaxed slightly. 'Also I doubt that Charlotte keeps to such rules.'

'No. She comes laden with presents every visit, including the suede jacket you gave to someone to put away.'

'You cannot hurt your dearest friend by refusing her as you refuse me.' Dante got up, holding out a hand to Rose as a waiter informed him their table was ready.

She was thoughtful as she accompanied him to a small, intimate dining room very different from the large one used for Charlotte's wedding breakfast. Had her refusal actually hurt Dante?

The room was full, the atmosphere lively with the buzz of conversation, and though not as loud as at the trattoria in Santa Croce a great improvement on the hushed elegance of her first dinner in Florence.

Dante nodded when Rose mentioned it. 'I was

surprised that Charlotte chose that particular hotel for your stay. You liked it there?'

'I was a bit intimidated when I first walked through the doors. But at the time I was so worried about Charlotte—' She halted, biting her lip.

'Fabio told me why,' Dante assured her quickly. 'Charlotte suspected him of taking some other woman to New York on their wedding anniversary. *Incredibile*!' He shook his head. 'There are many men who do such things, of course, but Fabio Vilari, never. And now Charlotte is about to give him a child he is the happiest man alive. What will you drink, Rose?'

'No more wine for me, thanks. I'll have some lovely Welsh water.'

'Because I will drive you home I will drink the same.'

'If you send me back in a taxi you won't have to.'

Dante glared at her. 'You think I would do that so I could drink another glass of wine?'

'Just a thought,' she murmured as they were served with miniature Welsh rarebits.

From then on Rose made sure she was as good company as possible as they ate their appetisers and then watched, impressed, as a huge roast of beef was carved on a trolley at the table and perfect high-rise Yorkshire puddings served to them with locally grown vegetables.

'Do you cook roast beef like this, Rose?' asked Dante as they began eating.

'I've never tried,' she confessed. 'Mum does it on Sundays sometimes, but usually goes for roast chicken, Bea's favourite. At home I cook pasta a lot—and, of course, the inevitable fish fingers, which my daughter would eat every day if allowed.'

'You make the pasta?'

'Alas, no. I buy the fresh kind from a supermarket. But I do make my own sauces.' Rose smiled at him as she went on with her meal. 'I see why you always order this here, Dante. It's superb.'

'Yet I think you enjoyed our meals in Firenze also, yes?'

'I certainly did.' Her eyes met his. 'You made my little holiday there very special, Dante.'

He smiled warmly. '*Grazie*. It was special for me, too. You must come again soon. And this time, perhaps, you will bring your daughter?'

Rose suppressed a shiver at the thought as Dante

leaned nearer, the warmth of his breath on her cheek. 'I hope very much that you will come. You have forgiven me at last, Rose?'

'For coming to see me today?'

His eyes held hers. 'No. For leaving you here so suddenly all those years ago, when I wanted so much to stay.'

'Oh, that,' she said airily. 'Of course I have. For-given and forgotten years ago.'

Dante's smile was wry. 'You put me in my place, I think.'

Her eyes fell. 'Let's not talk about it any more, Dante. It was a long time ago and we're two dif-ferent people now.'

'*Certo,*' he agreed. 'You are the successful one with your own business and your beautiful daugh-ter—'

'While you help run the exalted Fortinari vine-yards.'

'But I made a bad marriage,' he said bitterly.

She shrugged. 'My record's hardly faultless in one instance.'

'You speak of Bea's father?' He frowned. 'Are you sure you will not search out this man and tell him about her?'

'Absolutely sure. Can we talk about something else, please?'

'I shall do whatever you wish, *carina*.'

Tony Mostyn joined them shortly afterwards for coffee. He showed them the latest photographs of his children and received the news that Rose was a single parent with much interest when Dante told him she ran her own business.

'When you take a day off you must bring your little girl over to meet Allegra and my two,' he told her. 'My wife would like that very much.'

Rose thanked him and looked at her watch. 'And now I'm afraid I must be getting home. It was a wonderful meal, Tony. My sincere compliments to the chef.'

'I'll pass them on.' Tony grinned at his cousin. 'Though next time try something different. Dante here always goes for the same thing.'

'Why not? I eat it nowhere else. Also it is your national dish and your man does it to perfection,' said Dante, unmoved. 'I shall see you in the morning, Tony, but now I must drive Rose home.'

To Rose's surprise, Tony Mostyn asked for her telephone number as they left, so he could get in touch when his wife came home.

'I like your cousin,' she said on the way to the car park.

'He is a great guy,' Dante agreed. 'You will like Allegra also.' He gave her a searching look as he helped her into the car. 'Will you visit her, Rose?'

'If she asks me to, yes, I will.' Rose found she liked the idea a lot. She'd lost touch with most of the friends she'd made in college, mainly because they were now pursuing high-profile careers, or if they had children they also had a husband. And Charlotte, her closest friend of all, lived in Italy.

'You enjoyed the evening, Rose?' asked Dante as he drove off.

'Very much. Thank you for taking me there.'

'Even though it was where we first met?'

'Even so.'

When they arrived at Willow House, Dante switched off the ignition and gave Rose a wry sidelong glance. 'This is where we say goodbye, unless you will invite me in to talk for a while before we part.'

Rose nodded. It was relatively early, and who knew when she would have another evening like this? 'I could make more coffee—'

'I have no wish for more coffee,' he said and smiled. 'But I would very much like more of your company.'

CHAPTER FOUR

ROSE UNLOCKED HER front door and led Dante into the small sitting room, which was unusually tidy, partly due to Bea's absence, and partly because Rose had whirled round it like a dervish in case Dante came in when they arrived home. She took off her jacket and laid it on the back of a chair.

'Are you sure you won't have coffee?' she said, suddenly awkward now they were alone together in the silent house.

He shook his head and took her hand to draw her down on the comfortable velvet sofa that dated from Rose's childhood. 'This is a very warm, welcoming room,' said Dante, surveying it appreciatively.

'All my mother's work,' she assured him. 'I'm lucky. Not many single parents own a fully furnished home, complete with willing babysitters close at hand.'

'Davvero!' Dante smoothed a hand over the up-

holstery. 'There is a sofa a little like this in my house also, Rose. My grandmother was fond of velvet.'

'Have you kept all her furniture?'

'Yes.' He sighed. 'At first I thought this was a mistake. I kept waiting for Nonna to walk through the door to join me. But now, every time I go home I feel her warmth and love welcoming me.'

'Your wife didn't feel the same about it, obviously,' Rose said, and wished she hadn't as his face hardened into a mask.

'I do not like to discuss her,' he said, looking down his nose.

She nodded coldly. 'How true. You certainly made no mention of her the first time we met.'

'I have apologised for this already, more than once,' he said wearily and got up. 'I think it is best I leave.'

Rose jumped to her feet, chin lifted. 'So leave.'

For a moment she was sure that Dante, his eyes blazing blue flames, was about to storm out of the house there and then, but with a choked sound he pulled her into his arms and kissed her fiercely. *'Arrivederci, tesoro.'*

By supreme effort of will Rose detached herself, her eyes glittering hotly. 'That's what you said last time.'

He frowned. 'At the airport in Pisa?'

'No. When you left my bed after the wedding.' She smiled sweetly. 'Goodbye, Dante. Thank you for dinner.'

'Tell me, Rose,' he demanded angrily, 'why did you accept my invitation tonight? At one moment I think we are friends, but then in the blink of the eye I am enemy again.' His eyes narrowed. 'It amazes me that you agreed to my company in Firenze.'

It had amazed Rose at the time. 'I was alone in a foreign country, remember?' She eyed him narrowly. 'If it comes to that, why did you offer? Did Charlotte ask you to take pity on me?'

Dante looked down his nose again. 'I felt pity without being asked.'

Rose glared at him, incensed. 'So Saint Dante escorted Charlotte's little friend out of the goodness of his heart!'

He raised a shoulder. 'You could say that, yes. Though I am no saint.'

'No. Neither am I. As you have discovered for yourself since meeting up with me again, my disposition has deteriorated.' She felt sudden shame. 'So have my manners.'

Dante's smile stopped short of his eyes. 'You have reason. You work hard with no husband to provide for your daughter, and you do well. She is a credit to you.'

'But Bea has a temper, too, which is definitely down to me, because her father—' She stopped dead at the sharp look Dante gave her.

'Her father is of better disposition?'

She nodded, flushing.

'You know this from just one night?' he demanded. 'Rose, I think you know much more than that, so why do you not contact him? He deserves to know the truth.'

She took a leaf from Dante's book and stared down her nose at him. 'It's absolutely none of your business, Dante Fortinari.'

He stiffened, and inclined his head with hauteur. 'You are right. It is not. Goodbye, Rose.'

He strode from the room and straight out of the house. Rose gave a choked sob as she heard the outer door close, and then began to cry in earnest as Dante drove away. She curled up in a heap on the sofa, and for the first time in years gave way to engulfing, bitter tears that only died down at last when she remembered the dress. Head thumping, stomach suddenly unhappy after the rich dinner, she trudged upstairs, hung up her dress and pulled on her bathrobe. She took off her makeup and pressed a wet cloth to her swollen eyes then stiffened, heart hammering, at the sound of the doorbell. Rose raced down the stairs, almost falling in her haste to wrench open the door, and found Dante holding out something that caught the light.

'Your earring, Rose. It came off in the car, I think.'

'Oh. Thank you.' She swallowed convulsively, trying to blink away the black spots dancing in front of her eyes. 'Dante I'm…I'm so sorry, but—' She uttered a sick little moan and would have crumpled in a heap if he hadn't sprung to catch her.

Rose came round on the sofa with Dante leaning over her, an expression of desperate anxiety on his face as he bombarded her with a flood of questions she couldn't understand.

'English,' she croaked, and his eyes lit with a smile so brilliant she closed her own in defence.

'Forgive me, *bella*, in my panic my English deserted me. What is wrong?'

'I passed out.'

'*Certo*! But why?'

'I panicked when you rang the bell.'

'Ah, Rose. I am so sorry. Though it is not so very late.'

'I know. But my immediate thought was Bea. Mothers tend to be wired that way.'

Dante slid an arm beneath her and slowly and very carefully raised her to a sitting position. 'Your head still spins?'

Rose thought about it. 'A bit. Could you hang on to me a little longer?'

He muttered something under his breath.

'What did you say?'

'I will hold you all night if you permit.' He smiled. 'But I will not expect that.'

Her lips twitched. 'I won't, either. I meant until the room stands still.'

Dante sat beside her, holding her close. '*Allora*, you are comfortable like this?'

'Yes.' Much too comfortable.

He looked down into her swollen eyes. 'You

have been weeping, *cara*. Because we parted in anger?'

She nodded again and, to her dismay, her eyes filled again. 'And now my head is aching, and I look *awful*.'

'You do not,' he assured her, and gathered her closer. 'You need some of your tea, perhaps?'

Rose managed a smile. 'Do you know how to make tea, Dante?'

He shrugged. 'I put the tea-bag in the cup and pour the hot water, yes?'

'Absolutely. But I won't have any just now.' The scent and warmth and muscular security of his embrace were far more effective than tea. And, unlike tea, were not normal features of her life. 'Sorry I was such a shrew earlier. I enjoyed our evening, Dante. At least until the moment you stormed off and left me sobbing my heart out.'

Dante turned her face up to his. 'You cried because I left?'

'Yes.' She drew in a deep, shuddering breath. 'I was utterly horrible, and you didn't give me the chance to say I was sorry.'

His eyes held hers with a look which turned her

heart over. 'We have both made enough apologies now, *bella*, yes?'

She nodded, her bottom lip quivering as she tried to smile. 'Are we friends again?'

Before the words were out of her mouth, Dante's lips were on hers, and she gave herself up to his kiss with a relishing little sound that tightened his arms round her as he kissed her swollen eyelids and her red nose and then returned to her quivering parted mouth with a sigh of such pleasure she melted against him, shivering in response to his urgent, caressing hands. Emotions heightened by the quarrel, their kisses grew wild with such hunger that history repeated itself with inexorable rapture. Hands and lips came together as clothes flew in all directions, restraint gone up in smoke as they came together in a pulsating, overpowering rush of desire that hurled them both to orgasm, and left them panting and breathless, staring at each other in shock.

'*Dio,*' Dante said hoarsely at last. 'From the moment I saw you again in Firenze I have wanted this, but I swear I did not intend it tonight, *tesoro.*'

Rose pushed him away and suddenly hotly aware of her nakedness, snatched up her robe.

'My fault as much as yours, Dante.' She swallowed hard. 'I don't know what to say, so please go now.' Before she did something really insane and begged him to take her to bed and make love to her all night.

Dante pulled on his clothes at top speed and then turned to her, his blue eyes lambent with a light which sent a streak of heat right down to her toes. *'Arrivederci, amore.* But this is not goodbye. I shall return soon. Very soon.' He took her in his arms. 'I have no wish to leave you now, Rose, but it is late and you need your bed.'

She looked at him searchingly. 'Why did you come back, Dante?'

'Because nothing has changed since that first time we met,' he said huskily, smoothing a hand down her cheek as he released her. 'You are as irresistible to me now as you were then. *Buonanotte, carissima.'*

Rose watched him stride down the path to the car at the gate, wishing her heart would resume its normal beat. Dante turned to wave, and she lifted a shaking hand in return, then closed the door and went upstairs to stand under a hot shower to recover. Fool! How could she have allowed that to happen again? Allowed? She gave a mirthless laugh. She could no more have prevented it than stopped breathing.

Grace had insisted on giving Bea her breakfast and then driving her to school so Rose could enjoy the added luxury of a lie-in the next morning, but Rose was showered and dressed and ready to start work by the time her mother called in before going home.

'I've made some coffee,' she said, smiling.

'Good. I need it.' Grace sat down at the kitchen table and watched her daughter filling cups.

'Was Bea all right last night, Mum?'

'Fine. How about you? Did Dante change your mind about going out?'

'Yes. We went to the Hermitage.' Rose set the cups on the table, eyeing her mother narrowly. 'What's wrong? Are you sure Bea didn't play up last night?'

'She was as good as gold.' Grace took a deep breath. 'Look, Rose, there's no easy way to say this, but it's time you told me the truth. Is Dante her father?'

'What?' Rose went cold. 'Why on earth should you think that?'

'Because,' continued Grace relentlessly, 'yesterday when Bea smiled at him and Dante smiled back, the resemblance stared me in the face, not least the blue eyes. Your father's eyes were dark like yours and mine. And I'd better warn you that Tom, not normally observant in such matters, commented on it first.'

'Which doesn't make it true.'

'Doesn't it? I couldn't sleep last night as I thought back to the wedding, how Tom and I preferred to drive home once Charlotte and Fabio left on their honeymoon, but booked a room for you so you could enjoy the party with the other guests. Then Dante Fortinari had to leave in a hurry because his grandmother was ill.'

'So you think he somehow sandwiched in a quickie with me before he took off?' snapped Rose.

Her mother winced. 'I wouldn't have put it quite like that, but it would certainly explain a lot.' Her eyes remained locked with her daughter's. 'I'm right, aren't I?'

The backbone Rose had always managed to keep so rigid suddenly crumbled. Unable to look away, she slumped down on a kitchen chair. 'Yes, you are. But this doesn't change anything. I have absolutely no intention of telling Dante.'

'Why not?' Grace reached to take her hand. 'Can you tell me what happened after we left that night, darling?'

Rose nodded reluctantly.

She had been dancing to something slow with Dante late in the evening when it struck her that Charlotte's home would now be in Italy with Fabio, and her lifelong friendship with Rose would naturally take a back seat. When Dante had asked why she was sad she'd confided in him and blinked away her tears, suddenly desperate to get to bed. Dante had insisted on escorting her to her room, where he'd held her in his arms to comfort her, at which point she'd found she was no longer tired and within seconds they'd been kissing and caressing wildly, shedding their clothes to fall on the bed and join together in a maelstrom of heart-stopping bliss. They had still been locked in each other's arms, breathless as they came back to earth, when Dante's phone rang. Cursing, he had reached over Rose to pick it up, then with a wild exclamation he'd withdrawn to leap to his feet to dress, all the while continuing an impassioned conversation with the caller in Italian. Rose had pulled the sheet up to her chin as Dante, face ashen and haggard, begged forgiveness for his sudden departure, his English erratic in his distress as he explained he had to return home immediately because his grandmother was very ill. 'I will contact you soon. *Arrivederci, tesoro*,' had been the parting words she'd never forgotten.

She smiled bitterly. 'After he'd gone I lay in a rose-tinted afterglow, dreaming of a future relationship with Dante, only to discover the next morning that he had a fiancée he'd forgotten to mention.'

Grace winced. 'And you'd had unprotected sex!'

Rose gave a mirthless laugh. 'Not a bit of it. He used a condom, but it was faulty. In his rush to get away he didn't realise that, so I knew it was unlikely he'd believe he was the father of my child.' She eyed her mother ruefully. 'Not that it was possible to tell him, anyway. By the time I realised I was pregnant I was two months along, as you well know, and Dante Fortinari was well and truly married by then. So there was no way I could name him as Bea's father. Dante is one of Fabio's closest friends, and Fabio is married to *my* dearest friend, so I just couldn't spoil things for Charlotte and perhaps even risk affecting the relationship between you and Tom.'

'So you invented a one-night stand after a college party.' Grace got up and pulled her daughter into her arms. 'My darling girl, what are you going to do now?'

'Nothing.' Rose swallowed hard. 'I was such a fool to go to Florence. I'd been refusing to all this time just in case I met Dante again. And then Charlotte actually sent him to see me at the hotel, and I took one look at him and knew exactly why I'd fallen in love at first sight all those years ago. Because, Mum, if I hadn't fallen so hard for him it wouldn't have happened.' Her face flamed. 'And in case you're wondering, Dante was no way to blame. It was completely consensual.' Not only then but last night, too. Would she ever learn?

Grace stood back and looked at her daughter searchingly. 'Are you still in love with him?'

Rose nodded miserably. 'But I don't *want* to be. Part of me still blames him for what happened, and now and then my resentment gets the upper hand.'

'Did you part on good terms last night?'

'Eventually, yes. But there were a few awkward moments during the evening *and* when he brought me home. In fact, I offended Dante so much he drove off in a strop. But he drove back again later, so we were on good terms again before we said goodbye.' Far too good, damn him. 'It's a pity Bea inherited my disposition, not Dante's.'

Grace smiled wryly. 'He was very taken with her, love.'

Rose shivered. 'I know. But it makes no difference.'

'Are you really sure about that?'

'Yes, Mother.'

'But surely you must have considered telling Dante about Bea once you knew his marriage was over?'

'I didn't *know* it was over. I always refused to listen if Charlotte so much as mentioned Dante's name. You knew, obviously.'

Grace nodded. 'We met him on a visit to Charlotte, but when I tried to tell you about it you shut me up. I understand why now.'

Rose sighed. 'I wish I had listened to you, Mum. I put my foot in it with Dante the first night we met up again in Florence. When he suggested taking Charlotte's place at dinner I practically spat at him and asked if he was bringing his wife along. What a sweetheart I can be when I try!'

Grace gave her a hug. 'I love you just the same.'

When her mother went home Rose got down to work, and did her best to lose herself in it, but it was hard now Grace knew the truth. During the years when the identity of Bea's father had been her own private secret she had hidden it away like an oyster covering a grain of sand. But now it was a secret no longer. She hadn't thought to swear her mother to silence about it, and the relationship between Grace and Tom was so close he would soon know something was wrong and coax the truth out of her. Then probably Charlotte would be the next to know and now she was pregnant and hormonal she was unlikely to be calm and reasonable about it. Rose shuddered as she imagined Charlotte storming into Dante's house, demanding that he did the right thing—whatever that was.

Revelations apart, life went on for Rose in much the same way as usual for the next few days, except for nights disturbed by thoughts of the passionate encounter with Dante, and the fact that her daughter's parentage was no longer a secret. Grace assured her she had not confided in Tom, but found that very hard.

'It's your secret, not mine,' she said unhappily. 'I still think you're wrong to keep the truth from Dante. It would be much better to tell him yourself rather than have him discover it some other way.'

'There is no other way. You're the only one who knows, Mum.' Rose frowned. 'Though you said Tom commented on the likeness. Has he said anything?'

'Yes. But I told him he was imagining it, that Bea's blue eyes came from my grandmother.' Grace pulled a face. 'I just loathed lying to him, Rose.'

'But I'm grateful you did. Think about it! A single mother working hard to provide for her daughter suddenly informs wealthy scion of famous Fortinari wine-producing family that he's her child's father.' Rose's mouth twisted cynically at the thought.

But later than night, when Dante rang after she was in bed, Rose was sorely tempted to tell him the truth when he asked after her little daughter. 'You must be so proud of her. And how is her beautiful mother?' he asked in a tone so caressing Rose's toes curled under the covers.

'Working hard, but otherwise fine. How are you, Dante?'

'I am also working hard, but I cannot sleep for wanting you in my arms again. I need so much to see you, *tesoro*, but for a while this is not possible. I have seen Charlotte,' he added, 'and she is very well.'

'I'm so glad for her and for Fabio.'

'He is looking forward to fatherhood very much—*Dio*, how I envy him!'

A wave of such guilt swept over Rose it was almost like pain. 'You won't when he's walking the floor at night when the baby won't sleep,' she said, deliberately flippant, 'or will he hire a nurse? How do you arrange such things in your world?'

'My world is not so different from yours, Rose. Some people have such help, but if I had a child I would wish to be involved in the caring as much as possible.'

'Sorry, Dante, I must go,' she said breathlessly, 'I think I hear Bea.'

'Then run, little *mamma*. I will ring again soon. *Buonanotte*.'

Rose laid the phone down and slid out of bed to check on Bea, who, as she'd known perfectly well, was fast asleep with Pinocchio and Bear. With her blond curls tumbled over her forehead and the unmistakable blue eyes closed, there was no resemblance to her father at all. But awake it was so marked to Rose that as Bea grew older she had been afraid that everyone involved who knew Dante would some day make the connection. Lying awake afterwards, Rose kept hearing the note in Dante's voice when he spoke of envying Fabio. Her mother was right. It was time to tell Dante he was Bea's father before someone, somehow, got in first. He deserved the truth from her whether he believed her or not.

CHAPTER FIVE

ROSE WAS GLAD to be abnormally busy the following week, with more travelling than usual. By the time she'd played with Bea once she'd got home, given her a bath and shared her supper, then read to her until she slept, Rose was too tired for soul-searching.

Dante rang to inform her that the following week he would be in London again and would drive down to see her. 'I shall take you out to dinner, Rose, but this time you may choose the restaurant,' he assured her, and laughed softly. 'And I will not come too early.'

Rose braced herself. 'Actually, Dante, perhaps you'd like to come to supper here this time. I'll cook.'

'*Grazie*, I would like that very much,' he assured her, surprised. 'But do not tire yourself with cooking. We can send out for a meal.'

Rose rolled her eyes at a sudden vision of a designer-suited Dante surrounded by foil cartons. 'I'll think about it.'

'I cannot sleep at night for missing you. Have you missed me?'

'Yes,' said Rose simply.

'*Ottimo*, I am very happy to hear it. I will be with you at eight on Wednesday evening.'

'Come earlier than that if you like.'

'I like very much, but won't your Beatrice object?'

'No. Apparently she likes you much more than Stuart.'

'And who,' growled Dante, 'is Stuart?'

'An old school friend I go out with occasionally. Bea disapproves of him because he calls her "little girl".'

'So you allow this man to come to your house?'

'No. But we've met him in the town a couple of times. He feels uncomfortable around Bea and she's picked up on it.'

Dante chuckled. 'I will not be uncomfortable with her.'

Rose bit her lip as she closed her phone. He might change his mind about that once he knew the truth. But she would tell him this time, somehow. She had nothing to lose. If Dante refused to acknowledge Bea she was no worse off than before. Besides, she was only taking his advice. It was Dante who'd insisted Bea's father had a right to know.

Grace's reaction to Rose's decision was a mixture of pride and apprehension. 'At least I can now tell Tom. We can provide backup if you like, darling.'

'That's very brave of you, but this is between Dante and me. You can stand by to pick up the pieces if things go pear-shaped.' Rose smiled ruefully. 'I've always been afraid this would happen one day. Every time Bea smiled up at Charlotte and Fabio I was sure the penny would drop, but it never did.'

'Only because they haven't seen Bea and Dante together.'

'True. They're in for a shock.'

'Not as big a shock as Dante.' Grace patted her hand. 'Are you sure you want to handle this alone, Rose? I'm perfectly willing to play the outraged parent. After all, Dante had no right to seduce you when he was about to marry someone else.'

'Mum, he didn't *seduce* me. One minute he was

comforting me, the next minute we were so utterly desperate for each other we didn't even hear his phone ring straight away.' Rose sighed. 'He didn't want to answer it but I insisted, and you know the rest.'

Now she'd made her decision to tell Dante the truth Rose wished she could have done so right away instead of having to wait a week. None of her usual travelling was necessary for the time being, which enabled her to get through a lot of work at home and spend more time with Bea, who was delighted by the arrangement.

'But you like it when Gramma looks after you?'

Bea nodded vigorously. 'And Tom,' she assured her mother, and then gave Rose the smile exactly like her father's. 'But I love you best, Mummy.'

'I love you best, too,' said Rose, clearing her throat.

She was reading to Bea on the sitting room sofa later when the doorbell rang.

'Gramma!' cried the child, sliding down.

'I don't think so. She's gone shopping with Tom. Hold my hand while we see who it is.'

Rose opened the front door to find a vividly attractive brunette smiling at them.

'Rose Palmer? I'm Harriet Fortinari. Sorry to take you by surprise like this, but I'm on a fleeting visit to my mother so Dante suggested I look you up.' She leaned down to the child. 'You are Bea, of course. I've heard all about you.' She smiled so warmly she received one of Bea's sunniest smiles in response.

'How lovely to meet you. Do come in.' Rose ushered her guest inside. 'Dante said you were English, but I didn't realise you came from Pennington.'

Bea looked up at the visitor with far more welcome than she'd given Dante. 'Want a cuppa tea?' she asked hospitably.

'I'd love one, darling.' Harriet grinned at Rose. 'If that's all right with Mummy?'

Rose laughed. 'You're honoured. Bea doesn't offer tea to everyone.'

'So I gather from Dante!'

'Come into the sitting room; I won't be a minute.'

'I'd rather watch while you make it. Bea will show me where.'

'Let's take our guest to the kitchen, then, pet,'

said Rose, surprised to see her daughter take Harriet's hand.

'We had to come home from the park,' Bea informed their visitor. 'It rained. Want to see my paintings?'

Harriet assured her she'd like nothing better, and inspected the artwork in the kitchen with due respect while Rose made tea and took a cake from a tin.

'You're a very good artist, Bea—' a verdict which won another smile '—shall we sit here at the table?'

Bea nodded proudly. 'I don't need a high chair now.'

'Of course not. You're a big girl.'

Rose smiled warmly into Harriet's beautiful dark eyes. 'You've been speaking to Dante!'

'Have you got a little girl?' asked Bea.

'Yes, though she's a big girl, too. A bit bigger than you. Her name's Chiara. And I have a son, too; his name's Luca. I couldn't bring them with me because they're in school.'

'I go to school,' said Bea proudly.

'Would you like some cake, Harriet?' said Rose.

'Gramma and me made it,' confided Bea.

'I'd love some,' said Harriet, and sipped her tea with pleasure. 'Wonderful. I can never get tea to taste the same in Fortino.'

Rose loaded a tray. 'Shall we go back to the other room?'

'Let's make it easy and stay here. OK with you, Bea?'

The child nodded happily.

'It's kind of you to spare the time to visit us,' said Rose warmly.

'Charlotte Vilari suggested it first, seconded by Dante, who gave me your number,' said Harriet, and grinned. 'After which, nothing would have kept me away, of course. I should have rung you first, but I'm on a very short flying visit, so I seized the moment. I hope I'm not interrupting your work?'

'You're not, but it wouldn't matter if you were.' Rose smiled eagerly. 'You've seen Charlotte recently? How was she?'

'Blooming! But she told me to say you'll have to fly there to see her because Fabio refuses to let her travel right now.' Harriet looked at her expectantly. 'Will you go?'

'As soon as I can, yes.' Rose smiled at her daughter. 'You can get down now if you like, Bea.'

'Get Pinocchio.'

'Off you go then.'

Harriet smiled as Bea ran off. 'She's lovely. Enjoy her at this stage while you can. They grow up too fast.' She turned, suddenly serious. 'Look, Rose, while we're alone, I just want you to know that Dante had a really rough deal with his marriage. The family was delighted when Elsa the Witch left him but, although he hid it well, the rejection must have been a blow to his pride. Up to the death of his grandmother, whom we all adored, life had been kind to Dante. Then Nonna died, and he married Elsa. She had chased him mercilessly, desperate to marry a Fortinari, but once she had the ring on her finger she refused to have children. Soon afterwards, thank God, she met a man as old as the hills, but so filthy rich the delightful Elsa left Dante flat and took off with her sugar daddy.'

Rose nodded. 'He told me this when I was in Florence. But why are *you* telling me, Harriet?'

'Because I think Dante's lonely. He's no playboy. He works hard and loves his family. My children adore him. So do I. And he cares for you, Rose. Otherwise he wouldn't have asked me to call in on you. How do you feel about him?'

Rose flushed. 'I like him very much. We met years ago, actually, at Charlotte's wedding.'

'So she told me—' Harriet broke off, smiling as Bea ran into the room brandishing Pinocchio. 'Isn't he gorgeous?'

From then on Harriet Fortinari concentrated on Bea, and a few minutes later got up to leave. 'I must go. It's been lovely to meet you both. May I have a kiss, Bea?'

The child promptly held up her face, beaming as Harriet caught her in a hug and gave her a smacking kiss on both cheeks.

'Thank you so much for coming,' said Rose as they made for the door.

'And for the lecture?'

'Is that what it was?'

'I hope it didn't come across that way. I was just putting in a good word. When you come to visit Charlotte we must get together again. It was good to meet you, Rose.' Harriet dropped a quick kiss on her cheek and smiled down at Bea. 'It was lovely to meet you, too, darling. Goodbye.'

'Bye-bye,' said Bea, so sadly that Rose picked her up and cuddled her as they waved their visitor off.

When Dante rang that night Rose thanked him for sending his sister-in-law to see her. 'Bea was very taken with her. So was I.'

'*Bene*. I thought you might like to meet her.'

'She's very attractive.'

'And the light of my brother's life. It was fascinating to watch Leo falling in love with her when they first met. Before that it was the women who fell for him.'

'Is he as good-looking as you?'

Dante laughed. 'However I answer will be wrong. But Leo is an attractive man, yes.'

'So are you.'

'*Grazie*, Rose, I am glad you think so.' He breathed in deeply. 'I am very impatient to see you again, and not just to hold you in my arms again, but because you have invited me to supper.'

'You haven't tasted my cooking yet.'

'The food will not matter if I am with you, *tesoro*.'

'I bet you say that to all the girls.'

'You are wrong. The only ladies who cook for me are my mother, Mirella and Harriet.'

'And I'm sure they're experts. You're making me nervous. It's just a casual kitchen supper. Don't expect haute cuisine, Dante.'

'I will enjoy whatever you choose to give me, *carina*,' he said in a tone which curled her toes.

Rose would have been nervous enough about merely cooking a meal for Dante, but with the thoughts of their lovemaking fresh in her mind and the spectre of confession lurking to round off the meal she lived in a state of tension which gradually increased until on the day of the dinner she was wound so tight that Grace took Bea off to the park with Tom so Rose could make her preparations uninterrupted.

'We'll give Bea her supper, too,' said Grace as they left. 'And for heaven's sake give yourself time to get ready, and then sit down for five minutes doing nothing. Try to relax, love.'

'And don't forget,' added Tom with emphasis, 'we're just minutes away if you need us.'

Rose smiled sheepishly. 'I know. I let my inner

drama queen take over for a minute, but I'm all right now. After all, he can't eat me, can he?'

But when she opened the door to Dante later, for a moment he gave every indication of wanting to do just that. He said nothing for a moment, his eyes gleaming with a look which brought colour to the face which had been pale with tension most of the day. '*Buonasera*, Rose,' he said huskily, and took her by the shoulders to kiss her very thoroughly. 'You look lovelier every time I see you.'

Since Rose had deliberately dressed down in jeans and a by no means new Cambridge-blue sweater she was pleased to hear it. 'Charmer! Shall I take your jacket?'

Dante shrugged out of the butter-soft leather and handed it to her. '*Grazie*. Where is little Bea?'

'Having tea with my mother and Tom. They'll bring her back shortly. In the meantime, come into the kitchen, where I can keep an eye on dinner while I give you a drink.'

'Something smells very good, Rose!'

'It's my signature dish,' she said, handing him a bottle and an opener. 'Will you do the honours?'

Dante inspected the label and laughed. 'A Fortinari Classico! *Grazie tante*, Rose.'

'When he knew I was feeding you, Tom gave it to me.'

'A man of taste!'

'I hope it's suitable as a partner to chicken.'

He smiled at her as he removed the cork. 'You can drink it with anything you wish, *cara*. Will you drink some now?'

'Just half a glass. I must put Bea to bed before we eat.' Rose tensed as the doorbell rang, and then smiled brightly. 'There she is now.'

Dante was the only one at ease when Grace came in with Tom following behind with Bea in his arms. Once the greetings were over, Tom put Bea down and stood tall and formidable as he looked from the child to Dante.

'Over to you now, love,' he said to Rose.

Bea smiled up at Dante. 'Mummy made chicken for you.'

He smiled back. 'I am very lucky, yes?'

She nodded, eyeing him curiously. 'You talk funny.'

'Bea!' exclaimed Grace. 'That's not very polite.'

'But true,' said Dante, chuckling. 'I talk this way because I am Italian, not English like you, *piccola*.'

'Please don't translate,' said Rose swiftly. 'Bea's a big girl, remember.' She looked at Grace. 'Would you two like a glass of wine?'

'No, thanks,' said her mother hastily. 'I put a casserole in the oven so we must get back to it. Nice to meet you, Dante.'

'My pleasure, *signora*.' He turned to Tom. 'I saw your daughter yesterday, and she looks very well. You are thrilled to have a grandchild, yes?'

'I am indeed.' Tom bent to brush a kiss over Bea's curls. 'Though I look on this one as my own, too.'

Grace gave her grandchild a kiss, then blew one to Rose and Dante and hurried Tom away.

'Signor Morley does not approve of me?' said Dante, frowning.

'Of course he does.' Rose looked down to see Bea eyeing Dante in speculation.

'Bath time,' she announced.

He smiled. 'Then perhaps I shall see you later when you are ready for bed.'

Bea looked at her mother. 'I want to show him my ducks.'

'Are you up for that, Dante?' asked Rose.

'I am honoured,' he assured her and smiled down at Bea. 'You have many ducks?'

She nodded importantly. 'Lots and lots.' She held up her arms to him. 'Up,' she ordered, then intercepted a look from her mother and dazzled Dante with her most winning smile. 'Please?'

He lifted her in the practised way of a man used to small children. 'So tell me where to go, *per favore*—that is how I say please,' he informed her.

Rose checked that all was well in the oven and then followed Bea and Dante upstairs to the small bathroom, which felt even smaller with the three of them inside it.

'Down now,' said Bea as her mother turned on the taps. She took a jar from the side of the bath and shook it. 'Bubbles,' she informed Dante. 'You do it.'

Dante smiled, entranced, as he obeyed, then widened his eyes in mock awe when Bea showed him a basket piled with rubber ducks. 'You were right, *piccola*, you have many, many ducks.'

'Right then,' said Rose briskly. 'Clothes off, Bea.'

Dante backed away. 'I will leave now.'

'No!' ordered Bea. 'Play with me.'

'She likes races with the ducks,' said Rose, 'but be careful or you'll be soaked.'

He smiled. '*Non importa.* I have been wet many times bathing Leo's children; Mirella's also.'

After a spirited session with a chortling Bea and a flotilla of ducks, Dante's hair was wet and his sweater so damp Rose took it away to put it in the dryer, and returned with an old sweatshirt acquired from one of her rugby-playing friends in college. 'This will have to do for a while, I'm afraid,' she said, averting her eyes from his muscular bronzed chest. 'Time to come out, Bea.'

'Mummy reads stories now,' the child told Dante as Rose enveloped her in a bath towel.

'You are a lucky girl,' he told her. 'No one reads stories to me.'

She chuckled, shaking her damp curls. 'You're too big.'

'True.' He glanced down at Rose, who was rubbing so hard her child protested. 'Do you think Mummy will let me listen while she reads to you?'

'A'course,' said Bea firmly.

'Then I will wait downstairs until you are ready,' said Dante.

'I'll call down when we are,' Rose told him, willing her stomach to stop churning.

Bea was so impatient to get the drying session over that Rose was feeling even more twitchy by the time her child was propped up in bed with Pinocchio and Bear.

'Call the man now,' said Bea imperiously, but then bit her lip at her mother's raised eyebrows. 'Please,' she muttered.

'I should think so. And our visitor's name is Dante. Can you say that?'

'A'course,' was the scornful answer.

Rose went out on the landing to call down. 'You can come up now, Dante.'

'Grazie.' He ran up the stairs two at a time and planted a kiss on her lips on the way into Bea's bedroom.

Bea had a story-book waiting open on the bed and waved a gracious hand at the basket chair drawn up close by. 'There, Dante—please.'

Dante's eyes, which had widened at his name, were luminous as they rested on the child, who looked like a Botticelli angel with the lamplight haloing her bright curls. 'You are most kind, *piccola*. Which story have you chosen?'

'*Goldilocks.*' Bea wriggled more comfortably against her pillows and smiled as Rose perched on the bed beside her. 'Ready, Mummy.'

Rose was proud of her steady voice as she read the story with the animation her daughter always demanded, with a different voice for each bear and a special one for Goldilocks. As she read, careful not to miss out a single word, it occurred to her that, though none of this had been planned, it was a good warm-up to her big announcement. Dante was obviously delighting in the interlude as he sat perfectly still, more handsome than a man had a right to be, even in the incongruous old sweatshirt. His eyes remained on Bea's face as she drank in every word. Towards the end her eyelids began to droop and when Rose finally closed the book the child made no protest when her mother kissed her good-night.

Dante got up very quietly, a look on his face which told Rose he would have liked to kiss the child, too, but he merely said a very quiet good night and left the room as Rose dimmed the lamp.

Before going down to join him, Rose took a detour to her room to tidy her hair and touch up her face, then ran down to open the dryer. 'I hope you're not sorry I asked you here to dinner now,' she said lightly as she handed his sweater to him. 'Bath time can be an exhausting experience.'

He stripped off the sweatshirt and pulled on the jersey. '*Grazie*, Rose. For you, bath time with Bea comes at the end of your working day, when you are already tired. For me, tonight, it was pure pleasure. Thank you for letting me share it.'

'You're welcome. Will you pour the wine now while I check on our dinner?'

Dante sniffed in appreciation as Rose opened the oven. 'It smells good.' He filled two glasses and with a sigh of satisfaction sat down at the table she'd made festive with a bright green cloth and yellow candles in pottery holders. 'This is much better than a restaurant.'

'Even one as good as your cousin's?'

'Yes.' Dante eyed her flushed face with pleasure as she set a casserole dish on the table. 'Here we are alone with no waiters to intrude. But I can help if you allow.'

Rose shook her head and took a dish of roasted vegetables from the oven. 'No, thanks. All done.' She took the lid from the main dish. 'This is chicken and broccoli in a creamy sauce, finished off with a Parmesan cheese gratin in honour of my guest. Please help yourself.'

'First we make a toast,' said Dante and held up his glass to touch hers. 'To many more evenings like this.' He paid Rose's cooking the best compliment of all by rolling his eyes in ecstasy at the first bite, then clearing his plate and accepting seconds. 'I hope you were not expecting there to be leftovers.'

'No, indeed; I'm glad you enjoyed it. But no pudding, I'm afraid, though I can offer you cheese instead.'

'I rarely eat *dolces*,' he assured her, 'and tonight I have devoured so much of your chicken dish I can eat nothing more.'

Rose braced herself. Confession time loomed. 'In that case I'll just make some coffee to take into the sitting room.'

'While you do that I shall visit your bathroom,' he said matter-of-factly.

She blew out the candles and gathered up the used dishes in a tearing hurry. By the time Dante returned, she had the coffee tray ready and the dishwasher stacked, and could find nothing more to do to delay the inevitable. 'If you'll just take the tray, then.'

Dante eyed her closely as he complied. 'Something is wrong, Rose? Do not worry about little Bea. I took a look through her open door and she is sleeping peacefully.'

'Good.' Regretting the second glass of wine she'd downed for Dutch courage, Rose followed Dante into the sitting room and asked him to set the tray down on the table in front of the sofa.

When they were settled side by side with their coffee Dante eyed her expectantly. 'After such an excellent dinner we should be sitting here relaxed. But you are very tense, Rose. Will you tell me why?'

'Yes,' she said, resigned. 'I will. But I don't know where to start—'

Dante smiled. 'At the beginning is usually the best place, *tesoro*.'

She tensed at the endearment then took in a deep breath. 'Dante, if you'll think back to Charlotte's wedding, you made it plain from the start that you were attracted to me. I was thrilled and excited, and so instantly attracted to *you* I drank so much more champagne than I should have. I was tearful after Charlotte left with Fabio. You comforted me when you took me to my room and you know what happened next.'

Dante brought her hand to his lips. 'The entire day with you had been like the *preliminari* for me. Foreplay, yes? *Allora*, the moment I kissed you I was lost. I have no excuse for what followed. I was no schoolboy to lose control in such a way. But as the climax to that happy day, the joy I felt in your arms, Rose, was sweeter than anything I had experienced before. It was torture to tear myself away from you, even though I was in desperate worry over Nonna.' He sighed heavily. 'All that day I had banished Elsa from my mind, but later, on the flight home, I felt great guilt because I had not told you about her. When did you learn that I had a *fidanzata*?'

'The next morning, over breakfast. Your friends were worried that your grandmother's illness would affect your wedding.' Rose looked him in the eye. 'The word *wedding* hit me so hard I was numb for a while. Then my temper kicked in. I wanted to punch that face of yours until you weren't so handsome any more. Denied the satisfaction of that, I blocked you from my mind instead, deleted you from my life and refused to listen whenever Charlotte mentioned your name. So she soon gave up trying.'

'And you never knew that Elsa left me,' he said very quietly and took her cup to put it on the tray with his.

'No.'

He frowned. 'Yet Charlotte was most insistent I delivered her letter to you in person in Firenze.'

Rose nodded. 'Fabio sent money for me in the package so she needed someone to deliver it, and you just happened to be on the spot.'

Dante smiled wryly. 'I was most happy to do it, but thought you would refuse to speak to me.'

'I wanted to!'

'Yet you agreed to dine with me.'

She shrugged. 'The thought of eating alone in that rather grand hotel was so daunting I decided to make use of you instead. But why did you offer, Dante?'

'You looked so unhappy when you read Charlotte's letter I longed to take you in my arms and comfort you. Instead, I offered to take her place.' He looked at her steadily. 'You have more to tell me, I think?'

'I do.' Rose sat very erect. 'That was the pro- logue. Now we get to the main part. I've decided to take your advice, Dante.'

He frowned. 'What advice, *cara*?'

'To tell Bea's father he has a daughter.'

His eyes blazed in sudden, vehement denial. 'No! I no longer think this a good idea. Do not, Rose. He is probably married by now. You are right; after all this time he will not believe the child is his.'

Rose looked long and hard into the impassioned blue eyes. 'Is that how you would react in such circumstances, Dante?'

'I believe not. I hope I would not. How could any man be sure of his reaction to such news?'

'Now's your chance to find out.' She took in a deep breath. 'Bea is *your* child, Dante.'

He sat like a man turned to stone for several endless seconds, his eyes wild on hers.

'*Cosa*? What are you saying?' His bronze skin drained of all colour. 'It is not a thing to joke about.'

'It's no joke, I assure you. I'm deadly serious.'

'*Dio!*' Dante thrust a hand through his hair as

he eyed her incredulously. 'But, even so desperate to make love to you, I used protection that night.'

She flushed. 'It didn't work. After you'd gone I found it had split.'

'Then what you say is really true?'

'You honestly think it's something I would lie about?'

He shook his head in wonder. 'Beatrice is the result of our lovemaking that night.'

Rose sighed heavily. 'I don't blame you for doubting it. I couldn't believe it myself.'

'Why did you never tell me this before?' he demanded with sudden heat.

'How could I, Dante?' she snapped. 'You were already married by the time I found out. Which is why I was so obstinate about refusing to name the father. But, after seeing you and Bea together for the first time, my mother was sure it was you and said you had a right to know.' Rose slumped back against the sofa cushions. 'So now you do. But don't worry; I'm not asking anything of you.'

He glared at her, incensed. 'You tell me I have a daughter and think I will walk away?'

Rose hugged her arms across her chest, refusing to look at him. 'I don't expect anything from you,

Dante. Bea and I have managed perfectly well up to now without you. So by all means walk away if you want. I have no proof that she's your child. If this were a Gothic novel she'd have a birthmark or something to show she was yours, but—'

'I need no proof,' he said roughly and got up to pace the room. 'If you say she is mine I will believe you.'

'Will believe or do believe?' demanded Rose.

Dante turned on her angrily. 'Do not mock my command of English, *per favore.*'

Rose sat very still, gazing at him in such misery Dante sat beside her again and took her hand.

'Why do you look at me so?'

'It was very hard to tell you, Dante.'

'Perche?'

'I was afraid you wouldn't believe me. And it's over four years since that night so you might have forgotten all about it. And even if you did remember you could have thought I was telling you about Bea to get money.'

Dante clenched a fist, as though hanging on to every shred of his self-control. At last he turned to look Rose in the eye. 'I had forgotten nothing. When I saw you again in Firenze I was transported back to the Vilari wedding and my meeting with the entrancing girl who stole my heart.'

'The heart which already belonged to someone else,' Rose said bitterly.

He shook his head. 'Elsa never had my heart. She had no use for it. She wanted my name and my money. But there was less money than she expected. Financially, I was a great disappointment to her.'

'Did you love her?'

'I desired her when we first met. And she desired marriage to a Fortinari.' Dante's mouth twisted. *'Alla fine*—in the end—I was deeply grateful to Enrico Calvi for taking her from me.' He took Rose's hand in his. 'Now, let us talk of important things. How soon can we get married?'

CHAPTER SIX

'HOLD ON!' SHE shook her head decisively. 'That's not going to happen, Dante.'

'*Cosa?*' He pulled her to her feet and stood staring down at her. 'We made a child together—'

'But by accident, not because we were in a relationship.' Rose held her ground. 'I didn't tell you about Bea to force you to marry me, Dante. I don't want—or need—a husband.'

'But this is not all about you, Rose,' he flung at her. 'My daughter needs a father. Soon she will be old enough to ask why she lacks one, no? Other children will ask also. You have not considered this?'

'Are you serious? Of course I have!' She sighed wearily. 'I had no way of providing one for her, or even to meet a likely candidate because I had to work from home so I could always be there for her. Besides, I like being in charge of my own life—and of hers. If I married you, Dante, I suppose you would expect me to uproot us to live with you in Italy?'

'*Naturalmente*. I have a home ready for you, also a family who would welcome you,' he said swiftly.

Rose shook her head firmly. 'It's not the basis for a marriage, Dante.'

'You would find it so hard to be my wife?' he demanded, eyes glittering.

In some ways not hard at all, but that wasn't the point. She should, she knew, be grateful that he'd taken the news of his fatherhood so well, with none of the doubts she'd expected. 'I think it's a mistake to rush into anything, Dante,' she said at last. 'You need time to get used to the idea.'

Dante stood with long legs apart and arms folded as he stared down at her. 'If you do not marry me I will demand to spend time with my daughter,' he said harshly.

'Of course,' she said, secretly dismayed. 'But before we descend to bickering about it perhaps you'll listen to what I have to say?'

'*Allora*, talk, Rose.'

'I'm sorry. I shouldn't have been so abrupt with my objection.' She gazed at him in appeal. 'But you must see that we are, in effect, strangers,

Dante. Before we rush into something as bind
ing as marriage, it would be sensible to get to
know each other better.'

His eyes softened slightly. 'Is that how you feel,
Rose? That I am a stranger?' He raised an eyebrow. 'After what happened here between us the
last time, how can you say that?'

She felt her face flame. 'It's obvious that we—
we're compatible in that way.'

'Compatible!' He gave a mirthless laugh. 'If you
mean I want to crush you in my arms and kiss
you until you are helpless to refuse me, you are
right. Do not look like that,' he added. 'I will not
resort to—to physical coercion, this is right? Instead, I give you no choice. You will marry me
and make your home in Italy with me and with
our daughter.'

'Oh, will I?' Rose cried. 'Just because you've
suddenly discovered you're Bea's father doesn't
give you the right to turn our lives upside down.'

'You are wrong. It does,' he retorted, a look in
his eyes that sent her backing away. 'My child
must grow up knowing she has a father who loves
and cares for her. If you do not agree to marriage
you must share Bea with me. She will like my

house, and she will have cousins to play with her, also doting grandparents and uncles and aunts.' He shook his head in sudden wonder. 'I was resigned to the role of uncle. To discover now that I am a father, I feel great joy.' He glared at her. 'Also great frustration because the mother of my child will not marry me.'

Rose thrust a hand through her hair, her eyes troubled. 'Before I took a giant step like that I'd have to be sure that it would make Bea happy.'

Dante held her gaze in silence for a time and then took her hands in his. '*Allora*, this is what we do, Rose. I will go back to Fortino to talk to my brother, also to my parents. Then I will return here to stay at the Hermitage for a while to spend time with Bea. Later, you must bring her to stay at the Villa Castiglione for a holiday to meet my family.' Dante's eyes held hers. 'You agree with this?'

She thought it over then nodded reluctantly.

'*Va bene.* But first she must be told I am her father.' He closed his eyes suddenly. '*Dio*, I still cannot believe it.'

'If you have any doubts on the subject say so now and we forget the whole thing,' said Rose and backed away as his eyes flew open to blaze into hers.

'I meant,' he said very deliberately, as though he was translating as he advanced on her, 'that I cannot believe my good fortune in possessing this child we created together.'

'By accident!' She stood her ground and met his eyes squarely. 'If we did marry would you expect more children?'

'I would hope for them, yes. So if you have some strange idea of a *matrimonio di convenienza*, put it from your mind. You would share my life. And my bed.' Dante drew her into his arms. 'Would that be so hard to do?'

'No,' she admitted, colouring. 'As you well know, Dante.'

He smiled victoriously and brushed his lips in a feather-light kiss over hers, then stiffened at the sound of an anguished cry upstairs.

Rose bolted away from him to take the stairs at a run, Dante hot on her heels as they raced into Bea's room to find her sitting on the floor beside her bed, crying piteously as she reached out her arms to her mother.

Rose scooped her up and ran with her to the

bathroom, where Bea threw up copiously. 'On the bed too,' she sobbed, and Rose held her close, murmuring wordless comfort as she glanced round to see what Dante was doing, her eyes scornful when she saw he'd vanished. Fair weather daddy!

But Dante reappeared in the doorway with an armful of bed linen. 'I took these from the bed and shall put them downstairs. Tell me where to find clean sheets, Rose.'

'Airing cupboard on the landing,' she said, startled. 'Bea's things are on the upper shelves.'

Dante eyed the bowed curly head with sympathy. '*Poverina*! Are you better now?'

Bea shook her head mournfully. 'My tummy hurts.'

'You will soon be better in a warm, clean bed,' he assured her.

By the time Bea was bathed, sans ducks this time, and fragrant in clean pyjamas, Dante had made her bed, complete with Pinocchio and Bear.

'A man of many talents,' murmured Rose as she tucked her daughter in.

'Dante, read to me,' commanded Bea, and smiled at him. 'Please?'

Rose blinked hard at the look on his face, and

turned away to sort through some books. 'How about *Pinocchio*?' she suggested, clearing her throat. 'He's Italian, too.'

'A good choice,' said Dante huskily as his daughter nodded in approval. 'Where shall I sit?'

'On the bed,' said Bea, and wriggled back against her pillows.

'I'll pop downstairs and get a drink,' said Rose, and escaped before she did something really stupid like bursting into tears at the sight of Bea with the father she didn't know she possessed.

Rose loaded the washing machine with Bea's sheets and pyjamas and stripped off her sweater, which had suffered in the interlude in the bathroom. She pulled on a T-shirt from the basket of laundry waiting to be ironed and went up to Bea's bedroom, but paused in the doorway, her throat tightening as she heard Dante's voice growing gradually softer as he read his daughter back to sleep. Rose stood very still as he finally closed the book and leaned down to brush a kiss over the bright curls. He turned and held a finger to his lips as he followed her downstairs.

Rose felt suddenly awkward, unsure what to do

or say next. 'Would you like some coffee, Dante, or maybe a drink?'

'Coffee, *per favore*, to wake myself up to drive. I almost sent myself to sleep with Bea,' he added wryly. 'I will come into the kitchen while you make it, Rose, then I must leave.'

'Thank you for your help,' she said as she filled the kettle. 'I was impressed.'

'I have helped in such ways before,' he said matter-of-factly. 'Perhaps the little one's *nonna* allowed too rich a *dolce* after supper.'

'Actually, Mum's pretty strict. But Tom isn't, so maybe Bea conned him into giving her an extra sweetie or two.' Rose smiled. 'He's putty in her hands.'

'Putty? Ah, yes, *stucco*. I sympathise. It must be hard to refuse her anything she desires.' Dante chuckled. 'He will find it even harder with Charlotte's child.'

When they sat facing each other across the kitchen table with mugs of coffee steaming between them, Rose smiled wryly. 'I thought Italian men were spoiled by *mammas* who did everything for them, yet you were very efficient tonight. Thank you.'

Dante shrugged. 'At home, when young, in Fortino, where my mother was very much in charge, I did little, I confess. Now I do many things for myself. After Elsa left me my family bombarded me with dinner invitations.' He smiled derisively. 'I wished only to be left alone but this was never allowed.'

'Your family obviously love you very much—'

'They will love you and little Bea also,' he said emphatically and reached a hand across to grasp hers, but released it and got up when Rose stiffened. 'I will go now and let you sleep.'

Rose walked to the door with Dante, her mind in turmoil. Half of her wanted nothing more than to creep into bed and pull the covers over her head. The other half, the part of her savouring the warmth and scent of Dante as they stood together, wanted to pull him into bed with her and blot out the world.

'Tell me the truth, Dante—how do you feel?' she asked. 'Now I've told you about Bea, I mean.'

'Amazed, but happy,' he said simply, and took her in his arms. 'I will be even happier when you are my wife, Rose. It is useless to fight. It is your fate. We were meant to be together.' He kissed the mouth which opened to protest and let her go. *'Arrivederci, tesoro.'*

Rose watched him stride down the path to the car, then closed the door and leaned against it for a moment, feeling limp. She pushed away from the door in sudden irritation—time to stop behaving like a character in a romantic movie and do her nightly chores. She had work to do tomorrow. As usual. But maybe a day off would be good for once. She was well in hand with the accounts she did at home and had no visits to make next day. Her mother would be desperate to hear how things had gone tonight, so after she took Bea to school in the morning—so long as she wasn't unwell again—Rose decided she would give Grace a full report over coffee.

To Rose's relief, Bea slept the night through and was even more bouncy than usual the next morning as she ate her cereal.

'I like Dante,' she announced when she'd finished.

Rose's stomach did a forward roll. 'Do you, darling?'

Bea nodded. 'Can he read stories again?'

'I expect so.'

'You like him, too, Mummy,' Bea stated.

'Yes, I do. Now, let's get a move on or we'll be late.'

When Rose got back home from the school run Grace had let herself in and had coffee waiting.

She eyed her daughter anxiously. 'You obviously had a bad night. Dante didn't believe you?'

Rose busied herself with filling mugs. 'Oh, he believed me right enough. He was stunned at first, but when the truth finally sank in he was all for marrying me right away.'

Grace's delighted smile faded quickly. 'But you don't want that.'

'No. As I told Dante, we're virtually strangers. Before jumping in at the deep end I made it clear we would need to know each other better, and I would have to be utterly sure that Bea was happy with the idea.'

'Did he agree?'

'Yes. He immediately made plans to go back to Fortino to arrange some leave, and then come back to stay at the Hermitage to spend time with his daughter.'

'Goodness,' said Grace, blinking. 'I take it you're against the idea?'

Rose nodded vehemently. 'The minute I gave Dante the good news he started giving orders. I was to change my life completely, marry him and take off for Italy to live with him and Bea in his house—the Villa Castiglione, left to him by his grandmother.'

Grace downed her own coffee and got up to re-fill their cups. 'Good for Dante. After all, love, he could have rejected all idea of Bea's paternity.'

'No chance of that; he was entranced with her from the start,' said Rose moodily. 'He played with her ducks with her in the bath, and after-wards sat with her while I read the bedtime story. Then I softened him up even more by giving him a good dinner before breaking the news that Bea was his child.'

'How did he take it?'

Rose blew out her cheeks. 'As I told you, once the truth sank in he ordered me to marry him. Then when I didn't joyfully and gratefully accept he turned belligerent and demanded time with his daughter whether I married him or not.'

'To take her to his place in Tuscany, you mean?' said Grace, startled. 'So what did you say?'

'Bea started crying at that point because she'd thrown up and we both bolted upstairs.'

'How did Dante cope with that?'

'He stripped the bed and remade it while I cleaned Bea up, then he read her to sleep.'

Grace smiled. 'Bravo, Dante! Tell me, darling, quite apart from Bea, how do you feel towards him now? Are you still bitter?'

Rose shook her head hopelessly. 'Fool that I am, I *love* him. I always have. I tried so hard to forget him, but it was impossible with Bea looking up at me with those eyes of his.'

'How does he feel about you?'

'I wish I knew. He still fancies me. Physically, I mean. But that's not enough for marriage, especially with people from such different backgrounds.'

'It works for Charlotte and Fabio,' Grace pointed out.

'True. But they got married because they really love each other. Dante's motive for marrying me is purely to get Bea.' Rose shivered. 'Last night, when I didn't leap at the marriage idea, he said he'd demand time with his daughter. Could he do that legally, do you think?'

'No idea. You didn't name him as her father on the birth certificate and you've never lived together. Also he's not a British national, so I should think it's unlikely. I'll ask Tom.'

'Dante thinks Tom doesn't approve of him.'

'He's right. Tom can't get past the fact that Dante made you pregnant when he was about to marry someone else.' Grace smiled wryly. 'Yet at the same time he can't help liking Dante either.'

Rose nodded ruefully. 'I know the feeling!'

'Have a cup of tea, then go off to bed for a bit. Tom and I will collect Bea.'

'That sounds wonderful. I didn't sleep much last night after all the excitement.' Rose hugged her mother. 'You spoil me.'

'I prefer to think of it as helping. Take a hot shower and climb into bed. I'll give Bea her lunch before bringing her home.' Grace kissed her weary daughter and pointed her at the door. 'Go.'

Rose felt better after the shower, and even managed a short nap. When she got up, she had come to a decision. This afternoon she would take Bea to the park, and then play all her favourite games with her and later watch her favourite cartoon film with her for the umpteenth time. Rose's teeth clenched. Bea didn't *need* a father! She'd done perfectly well without one up to now, and even had the benefit of a male presence in her life in the shape of Tom Morley.

When Dante rang that night, Rose was ready and armed, waiting for him.

'How are you tonight, *carina*?' he asked in the deep caressing tones which still had the power to raise the hairs on the back of her neck—something that infuriated her in the present circumstances. 'And how is my little Bea? Is she recovered now?'

'*My* little Bea, actually, and we're both fine.'

Silence for a moment. 'What is wrong, Rose?'

'I'm afraid the deal's off, Dante. I'm saying no to your demands.'

'*Cosa? Perche*? What has happened?'

'I've given it careful consideration and decided I can't face the upheaval of making a new life in a strange country. I like my life the way it is. There's no room for a man in it, even one as irresistible as Dante Fortinari,' she added with sarcasm.

'And so you will deprive me of my daughter,

and Bea of a father? Can you think only of yourself?' he demanded hotly.

Rose suddenly lost it. 'I had to after you left me pregnant and took off to marry someone else,' she spat at him. 'Goodbye, Dante.'

Dante tried ringing back several times but eventually gave up, which made her even more furious. When her phone rang an hour or so later she snatched it up, ready to tell Dante to go to hell until she saw the caller ID.

'When, Rose Palmer,' Charlotte said belligerently, 'were you going to tell *me* that Dante is Bea's father? I had to hear it from Dad.'

'I didn't tell Dante until last night, so you were next on the list. Not even Mum knew, so don't get angry with me.' Rose's voice broke. 'Please.'

'Oh, love, don't cry; of course I won't! But I demand details.'

'First of all, how are you feeling?'

'At this time of night I feel fine; in the mornings not so much. But never mind all that. You said Bea's daddy was some student, while all the time it was Fabio's best friend! So go on. Talk.'

With a sigh, Rose went through her story yet

again, with Charlotte exclaiming in amazement at intervals.

'You were so *brave*, Rose, going through all that and never telling a soul, and all the while working so hard to make a living for Bea. Though, thinking back, the clues were there. You would never listen if Dante's name came up, but I thought that was because of Elsa the Witch. I suppose he never mentioned her when he was charming the socks off my bridesmaid?'

'Of course not,' said Rose indignantly. 'Otherwise—'

'You'd have sent him packing! So now he knows about Bea, what happens next?'

'I am ordered to marry him and take Bea to live with him at his villa.'

'How masterful!' Charlotte waited for a moment then sighed. 'But you're not going to do that.'

'No. With help from my wonderful mother and your equally wonderful father, I've managed my life very well up to now. Dante can issue orders as much as he likes, but I'm staying put. And so is Bea.'

'Damn! I wish I could nip over and see you, but Fabio is adamant about no travelling for a while.

And, if I'm honest, I'm not up to it right now, anyway. If I send you the fares will you bring Bea here instead?'

The mere thought of being anywhere in the vicinity of Dante Fortinari made Rose want to kick and scream. 'I can't just now, love. Maybe later on.'

Rose checked on Bea and then stacked her pillows and got into bed to lean against them, waiting for the phone to ring. When it remained obdurately silent she removed two of the pillows and tried to settle down to sleep. Instead of issuing orders, all Dante had needed to get her consent was to tell her—and convince her—that he wanted to marry her because he loved her, not because she came as a package deal with their daughter.

When the phone rang later Rose shot upright and grabbed it, then sank back against the pillows when she saw the caller ID.

'You took a long time to pick up,' said Grace.

'I thought it was Dante again.'

'I gather you won't answer when he rings.'

'How do you gather?'

'Because he rang Tom—he got the number from

Fabio—and asked to speak to me. He's desperately worried about you, love.'

'Good!' said Rose viciously.

'I assured him that, healthwise, both you and Bea were fine, and told him it was best he doesn't contact you for a while.'

'And what did he say to that?'

'That he would try to take my advice, but it would be hard.'

'You should have told him not to contact me at all. Ever.'

Grace shook her head. 'I didn't do that because I know you only too well, Rose Palmer. If I had, you'd be utterly miserable. So I gave you the chance to change your mind when your temper dies down, as it always does, in time.'

'This wasn't a childish tantrum, Mum!'

'I know that. I also heard the pain in Dante's voice, love. When he does ring again, promise me you'll speak to him.'

'I'll think about it.'

This was a promise all too easy to keep. It was impossible for Rose to think about anything else. The nights were the worst part, just as they'd been years before, after her first encounter with Dante

Fortinari. Even though she immersed herself in her work and spent the rest of the time with Bea, she existed in a constant state of tension, waiting for a phone call from Dante. A phone call which never came.

CHAPTER SEVEN

IT WAS A relief to spend most of the following Sunday at Tom's house. Bea enjoyed her day so much she protested loudly when it was time to go home. She even refused to wave bye-bye to Gramma and Tom and sobbed when she was secured into her car seat for the drive home, but, much to Rose's relief, fell asleep once the car was in motion.

'Wake up, Bea. We're home now,' said Rose as she turned into the drive, then swallowed, her heart thumping, as she saw a familiar male figure standing on her front porch.

Dante strode forward to help, arms outstretched, as Rose unstrapped Bea. 'I will take her.'

Exhausted after a day spent trying to fool her mother and Tom that she was perfectly happy, Rose yielded his daughter to him without protest.

'This is a surprise,' she said coldly.

'We need to talk; you will not take my telephone calls, so I came,' he informed her, then looked down tenderly as Bea woke up with a smile of delight when she realised who was holding her.

'Dante! Read stories?'

He chuckled. 'Of course, *piccola*.'

Rose unlocked the door and switched on lights. Now Dante was here, he might as well make himself useful. 'Would you take her straight upstairs, please?'

Once Bea was in bed later, flanked by Pinocchio and Bear, Rose handed Dante a selection of books for Bea to choose from, kissed her daughter good-night and, after a moment's indecision, left them to it.

The sitting room seemed small and chilly after the space and comfort of Tom's house. Shivering with nerves as much as cold, Rose switched on the electric fire and drew the curtains, then went to the kitchen to make coffee and took a tray into the sitting room.

Dante joined her soon afterwards. 'Bea is fast asleep,' he said and crossed to the fire to hold out his hands. 'It is cold tonight.'

'Would you care for some coffee?'

His lips curved wryly. 'Yes, Rose. *Grazie*.'

'Why the smile?' she asked as she poured.

'You are so polite.'

She set the pot down with a clatter. 'Only to hide how worried I feel about the reason for your sudden appearance.'

He lifted a shoulder. 'It is nothing to cause distress, Rose. Because my first proposal did not meet with your approval, I came to make a different proposition.'

Rose sat down suddenly. 'What do you have in mind?' If he had some idea about taking Bea away from her to stay in Italy for weeks at a time he could think again.

Dante joined her on the old velvet settee, careful, she noted, to leave a space between them. '*Ascolta*—listen to me, Rose. I feel much guilt that in the heat of passion after the Vilari wedding I took from you something impossible to replace.'

She raised an eyebrow. 'I wasn't a virgin, Dante! I'd had a steady boyfriend in college.'

Dante's lips tightened. 'I meant that by leaving you with child I robbed you of your youthful freedom.'

Rose nodded as she thought it over. 'I suppose you could say that. I certainly had to grow up in a hurry. But, to be fair, I was an equal partner in what happened between us.'

'But if you had known about Elsa you would not have been, no?'

'Absolutely not! I wanted to beat you up when I found out about her.' She ran the tip of her tongue over suddenly dry lips. 'But the possibility of consequences never occurred to me because you used protection, and even though I later realised there had been a problem with the condom I really thought the chances of anything happening were a million to one. It was a huge shock to find out I was pregnant. There was an equally huge fuss when I refused to name the father.'

Dante took her hand. 'Why did you refuse?'

'You were married by then, so what was the point? You're a close friend of Fabio Vilari, so no way was I going to upset Charlotte's newly wedded bliss by bringing your name into it. Anyway,' she added militantly, 'I was determined to take care of Bea myself.'

He nodded. 'And you have done so admirably. But now I shall help you care for her.'

She eyed him warily. 'How, exactly?'

Dante's grasp tightened. 'The best way is to

marry and give our child the love and security of a normal family.' He raised an eyebrow. 'But you do not want this. You value your independence too much.'

'Yes,' she admitted unwillingly.

'Even so, you must listen to my plan.'

'I'm listening.'

Dante smiled in approval. '*Va bene*. The plan is simple. Arrange your work to take time off, and then bring Bea to the Villa Castiglione for a little holiday. We can visit Charlotte and Fabio, also my family, *naturalmente*.' He paused. 'My mother is longing to meet her granddaughter, Rose.'

She bit her lip. 'I can't believe she's longing to meet *me*, Dante.'

'You are wrong. I have told her everything, and she has much sympathy for you, also admiration for the way you work so hard to support our daughter.'

My daughter, thought Rose fiercely.

'My house has several bedrooms. You are not required to share mine,' he assured her suavely. 'A week is all I ask, to see how Bea likes life Italian style.'

'Are you saying that if she does like it you'll expect me to let her stay with you there from time to time?'

'She is too young to do that without her mother.' Dante put a finger under Rose's chin and turned her face up to his. 'You would come with her.'

Her eyes fell from the searching blue gaze. 'And if she doesn't like it there?'

'Then I must spend time with her here.'

'You mean stay here in my house?' she demanded.

He gave a mirthless laugh. 'I do not hope for such a privilege. I shall stay at the Hermitage and come here to take her out.'

Rose stared at him in defeat. 'Very well,' she said dully. 'I'll bring her to Italy, but only for a week. I can't take more time off than that.'

'*Bene*. Let me know when you are free.' Dante stood up. 'I will arrange my diary to give me time with Bea. And with you, of course, Rose,' he added silkily.

'Thank you so much!'

'*Prego*. Now I must go.'

Rose went to the door with him. 'When do you fly back?'

'Early in the morning. This was a truly flying

visit. And I have much more travelling to do once I get back, but by road, for which I am grateful.'

'You prefer roaring around Italy in your car, I imagine.'

'What man would not?' He took her hand and bowed formally over it. *'Arrivederci,* Rose.'

'Goodbye.' She hesitated. 'Dante, I'm sorry you had to come all this way. I should have let you talk to me on the phone.'

He shrugged. 'It was worth it to gain time with my daughter.'

She winced, hoping he couldn't tell how much that hurt. 'But if I come—'

'When you both come!'

'All right, when we come, you must make it plain to your family beforehand that this is just a holiday. It doesn't mean I've agreed to anything permanent.'

Dante nodded, his eyes expressionless for once. *'Va bene.* It shall be as you wish. And if Bea likes it there at my home, what then?'

Her chin lifted. 'Let's take this one step at a time.'

'There is one step you must take before you bring Bea to the Villa Castiglione. You must tell her I am her father.' Dante took her by the shoulders, ignoring the hand that tried to push him away. 'Let us be truthful with each other, Rose.'

'I just wish you'd been truthful when we first met,' she snapped, her eyes stormy. She still couldn't get past Dante's deception in the past. The hurt was still raw for her.

'I did not lie,' he said huskily. 'With you in my arms, I forgot Elsa existed—'

'We spent a lot of time together that day before we reached that point. And while you might not have lied, you omitted to tell me you were engaged, which is as bad as lying.'

'*Davvero*! But it was such pleasure to laugh and dance with you, I could not spoil the day by mentioning Elsa.' He pulled her closer. 'I fell under your spell at first sight and went on falling deeper and deeper all that day, until I lost control as we kissed later in your room. It was such agony to leave you that, even frantic with worry over Nonna on the flight home, I was determined to tell Elsa I could not marry her. That I had met someone else.'

Rose stared at him in disbelief. 'You obviously didn't tell her,' she said at last.

'Ah, but I did.' His mouth twisted in distaste at the memory. 'It was a painful revelation to see someone so physically beautiful turn into a *strega* before my eyes. She spat at me that she was expecting my child, which, as she knew well, gave me no choice. Nonna died the next day and in my grief I felt only relief that Elsa abandoned her plans for a big church wedding. She arranged a hasty civil ceremony instead in her determination to become a Fortinari.'

'So what happened to the baby?' asked Rose, stunned.

'There was no baby. Elsa lied. On our wedding night, she told me there had never been a child and never would be.' He dropped his hands and turned away. 'I was an arrogant fool, she told me, to imagine she would ruin her figure that way, even more fool to think I could jilt Elsa Marino, the supermodel all men lusted after. I stared at this beautiful woman saying these ugly things and felt such revulsion I did not touch her that night or ever again.' He gave a mirthless laugh. 'People pitied me when she left me for another man, but I rejoiced.'

'You never told anyone the truth about this?'

'Only Leo. Therefore, Harriet must know also.' He turned to look at her. 'If I had known that *you* were expecting my child, Rose, nothing would have made me go through with the *farsa* of my wedding to Elsa.'

'You must have found it hard to live with her after that?'

His mouth tightened. 'I did not do so very much. With Leo's help, I made sure I was often away on my travels when she was home, which for Elsa meant her flat in Firenze. She hated the Villa Castiglione.'

'But you love it,' said Rose quietly.

'Very much. After Elsa left with Enrico Calvi— and my fervent blessing—the house was my sanctuary.'

'Yet your family tried to get you out of it as much as possible.'

'To show the world I was not heartbroken. My parents were enraged that Elsa had treated me in such a way. It was my mother's greatest wish that I find someone else as soon as possible.' He rolled his eyes. 'Therefore, every time I dined with my parents, or with Mirella and Franco, even Fabio and Charlotte, there was always some woman invited for me.'

'How about your brother?'

'Leo told me I could find my own woman, and Harriet lured me from my house by asking me to do the babysitting for them—which is when I learned to change a bed quickly! I enjoyed this much more than the socialising. But the one I am most grateful to is Charlotte Vilari. She sent me to Firenze to find you again, Rose.' He paused, his eyes searching hers. 'Are you truly sorry that I did?'

Rose eyed him thoughtfully. 'You really told Elsa the wedding was off because you'd met me?'

'Yes.' He raised a dark eyebrow. 'You do not believe me?'

'I want to,' she said honestly.

'But you still have doubts.' He stood back. '*Non importa.* I shall ring you next week to learn when you are free to leave. I will make the travel arrangements.'

'Right. I hope Bea will take to air travel.'

'With both of us to care for her, there will be no problem.'

Her eyes widened. 'You're coming to collect us?'

He smiled bleakly. 'This surprises you?'

'Well, yes; I expected to cope alone.'

'As always. If you prefer to do that—'

'*No*! Indeed, I don't. Thank you.'

'*Prego*. You will permit me to look in on Bea before I go?'

'Of course.'

Rose watched him leave the room with the swift grace that was such an essential part of Dante Fortinari and felt sudden regret, as though she'd somehow missed out on something important. She smiled brightly when he returned. 'Is Bea all right?'

'She is sleeping like an angel, as all children look when they sleep, even Luca, Leo's son, who is more demon than angel when awake. And now I must go. I will ring you early in the week.' His eyes locked on hers imperiously. 'And this time you will answer me and talk to me.'

'Yes, I will. And Dante,' she added quickly before she could change her mind, 'I'm not sorry.'

'*Cosa?*' He frowned.

'That you found me in Florence.'

'*Bene*, I am happy to hear it!' But, instead of kissing her as she'd hoped, he gave her the smile he shared with his daughter and turned to go. '*Arrivederci*, Rose.'

CHAPTER EIGHT

ONE OF THE highest of the several hurdles facing Rose was informing Bea that Dante was her
daddy. Grace advised doing it straight away before Dante rang again, so that evening, after reading a longer than usual bedtime story to put off the
moment, Rose finally told Bea she had exciting
news—they were going on holiday to Italy, where
Auntie Charlotte lived, to stay in Dante's house.

Bea, no lover of road journeys, frowned. 'In
the car?'

'Only for a little way. Dante is driving us to the
airport to catch an aeroplane.'

The blue eyes lit up. 'Tomorrow?'

'No, not tomorrow, darling, but soon.'

'Gramma and Tom, too?'

'No, just you and me. And Dante. Will you like
that?'

Bea nodded eagerly. 'Are there stories in his
house?'

'I don't know. We'll take ours, shall we?'

'OK.'

Rose took a deep breath. 'Darling, I've got a secret to tell you.'

'What?'

'Dante is your daddy.'

The blue eyes stared at her blankly for a moment then rounded like saucers. 'A real daddy, like Holly's?'

Rose cleared her throat. 'Yes.'

Bea was quiet for several long, tense moments. 'Will he get me from school?' she said at last.

Rose blinked, taken aback. 'Why, yes, I'm sure he will when he's here.'

Bea smiled triumphantly. 'Dante's *much* nicer than Holly's daddy.'

'You like him then?'

'Yes.' Another pause. 'Why didn't he come before?'

The question Rose had been dreading. 'I wouldn't let him.'

'Why?'

'Because I was silly.' Rose bent to kiss her. 'Now, go to sleep. You can tell Pinocchio and Bear your secret if you like.'

'And Gramma and Tom, too?'

'Yes. In the morning.'

After a hectic week spent in bringing accounts up to date and rearranging client appointments, Rose told Dante that the following week was good for her.

'*Ottimo.* I will make all arrangements and ring tomorrow with details.'

'Don't book a hotel room when you come to collect us,' she added casually. 'It would be more convenient to stay here the night before we leave—if you'd like to.'

He was silent for a moment. 'I would like that very much, Rose. *Grazie.* Is Bea happy about the trip?'

'She's wildly excited, though surprised that Gramma and Tom aren't going, too. I told her they had to do my job while we were away.'

He laughed. 'Is your mother happy to do that?'

'Yes, though I've tried to make sure there's very little for her to do.'

'You sound tired, Rose.'

'Nothing a night's sleep won't mend,' she assured him.

'I will ring as soon as I can. *Buonanotte.*'

Rose was in the middle of an endless ironing session when Dante rang to say he would be with her on Sunday afternoon and had arranged a flight to Pisa the following day.

'Is this good for you, Rose?'

'Yes, fine. Mum and Tom have taken Bea out so I can get our things ready.'

'They are much help to you.'

'Always. I'm very lucky.' She paused awkwardly. 'I'll see you tomorrow, then.'

'Yes, Rose. *A domani.*'

When Dante arrived next day Bea flew to the door to open it, beaming up at him. 'Dante, Dante. I've got a secret!'

'A secret! How exciting.' He put down his bag, smiling fondly as he picked her up. 'Will you share it with me?'

'Come inside first,' said Rose, peering past him down the drive. 'Where's your car?'

'I came by taxi.' He leaned to kiss her cheek. 'It is so good to be here, Rose. How are you?'

'I'm fine.'

'*Bene.*'

Dante followed her into the kitchen and sat down at the table with Bea on his lap. 'So, *piccola*, what is this wonderful secret?'

She beamed at him triumphantly. 'You're my real daddy!'

His eyes snapped shut as he hugged her close. 'That is such a wonderful secret. It makes me very happy,' he said when he could trust his voice. 'Does it make you happy?'

Bea nodded fervently. 'I told Gramma and Tom.'

Dante exchanged a look with Rose over the curly head. 'And did they like your secret?'

'Yes.' She looked up at him cajolingly. 'Will you get me from school now?'

'Like Holly's daddy,' explained Rose, busy with the coffee.

Dante took in a deep breath. 'I will like to do that very much, whenever your *mamma* says I may.'

Bea gave her mother a commanding look. 'Every day!'

'Dante doesn't live here, darling,' said Rose rather helplessly.

'But every time I come to England I will fetch you, *piccola*,' promised Dante, and speared Rose with a look which promised discussion on the subject later.

'Mummy was silly,' Bea informed him.

'Because I wouldn't let you come to see us until recently,' explained Rose, wishing she'd explained more to Dante before he came. But she'd been human enough to want to see his reaction when Bea told him her secret.

He smiled lovingly at his child. 'But now we are going to Italy together tomorrow to stay in my house.'

'Is it a big house?'

'Quite big, yes,' he said, ruffling her curls.

'You got children there?' she enquired.

Dante shook his head. 'You are my only child, *piccola*.'

'But you remember Harriet, the lovely lady who came to see us one day?' asked Rose.

Bea nodded with enthusiasm. 'She's got children.'

'You are so clever to remember,' said Dante proudly. 'Their daddy is my brother Leo, and we shall go to his house to play with Luca and Chiara.'

'Tomorrow?'

'No, but soon,' promised Dante. 'Tomorrow we fly in the aeroplane to Italy.'

Due to her excitement, Bea took longer to get to sleep than usual, and later, after a dinner shared with Dante in determined harmony, Rose's tension began to mount as she went upstairs ahead of him. 'You're in my room,' she informed him, ushering him inside. 'I hope you'll be comfortable.'

Dante closed the door quietly behind them. 'Where are you sleeping, Rose?'

'On the sofa bed in my study.'

He frowned. 'I should sleep there and you remain here, near to Bea, yes?'

'Certainly not. You wouldn't fit on it and, besides, I hear Bea wherever I am.' Rose made for the door, but Dante barred her way.

'I cannot take your bed, *cara*. But there is an obvious solution to the problem.' He took her in his arms. 'Share it with me.'

Rose opened her mouth to protest but Dante kissed her into silence. He held her hard against him and her body reacted involuntarily, savouring the scent of him and the pleasure of the contact with a taut, muscular, male body. He raised his head a fraction, but only to rub his cheek against hers and murmur in her ear in his own tongue.

'I don't understand,' she said hoarsely.

'Ah, but you do, *tesoro*,' he whispered. 'I desire you, Rose.'

Desire, not love, she thought bleakly.

Dante drew her closer, his lips against her cheek. 'I think—I know that you want me, yes?'

'Yes,' she admitted, but pulled away, blinking tears from her eyes. 'But not so much that I'll let you turn my life upside down again.'

'Ah, *carissima*, do not cry, or you'll break my heart.'

'Then you'll know how I felt when you broke mine!' Rose flung away and left the room, closing the door softly behind her.

Rose's second trip to Italy was very different from the first one. A chauffeured limousine replaced the coach trip to Heathrow, followed by a first-class flight to Pisa. The flight attendants were charmed with Bea, the females among them charmed with Dante, too, noted Rose acidly as she listened to melodic exchanges in Italian. She couldn't blame them. Dante was so obviously enjoying every minute of his time with his child, and so far Bea was behaving so well it was hard to remember she was prone to the odd tantrum or two at home. She was delighted with everything, including the pasta she was given for lunch, but Rose, occupied with thoughts of facing Dante's family, could only manage a cup of tea.

'You are not hungry?' asked Dante.

'No.' She managed a smile across her daughter's head. 'What happens when we land?'

'I shall drive you to the Villa Castiglione in my car. Do not worry,' he added. 'I have installed a car seat for Bea.'

'Thank you; how thoughtful,' said Rose, embarrassed because she hadn't thought of it herself.

To her gratitude, the rest of the flight passed quickly, helped by a peaceful interlude while Dante read to his daughter until she fell asleep. Rose sat, trying to relax, but her mind kept returning to the night before.

After her emotional parting shot, she had dreaded seeing Dante again this morning. To avoid him she'd showered and dressed hurriedly in the downstairs bathroom, and after getting Bea through the same process took the coward's way out by sending her to knock on Dante's door to say breakfast would be ready in a few minutes. She needn't have worried. Dante had walked into the kitchen later, smiling as though the biting little exchange of the night before had never happened. But his eyes had smudges of fatigue that matched hers.

Rose tensed as the plane began its descent. She wondered if Dante's family would be there *en masse* at his house to meet them, or if she'd have a day's grace to prepare herself while she explored the Villa Castiligione. A hand reached out to touch hers and she turned to face Dante's questioning eyes over his sleeping daughter's head.

'You feel ill, *cara*?'

'No, just nervous.'

'Of the landing?'

She shook her head. 'Of meeting your family.'

'You will not meet them today,' he assured her. 'I asked my parents to wait until tomorrow.' He smiled as Bea stirred. 'Wake up, *bella*. We are nearly there.'

They left the plane with much waving and hand kissing from the flight attendants for Bea. Dante would have picked her up to carry her but she shook her head.

'Walk—please.'

So Beatrice Grace Palmer made her entrance into the airport, hand in hand with both parents, her father carrying a shiny pink holdall with Pinocchio and Bear peeping out of it. As the trio reached the baggage carousel Rose saw a young man waving vigorously.

'*Va bene*, it is Tullio with my car keys,' Dante told Rose. 'He will help with the luggage.'

Tullio bowed, smiling, as Dante presented him to Rose and Bea, who grew very excited when she spotted her mother's familiar battered student luggage on the baggage carousel.

'Ours, Daddy,' she said, pointing.

Dante gave Rose a look which turned her heart over. 'So it is, *tesoro*,' he said huskily, 'and that is mine beside it.'

The useful Tullio helped stow the luggage in the car while Rose fastened her daughter into the smart scarlet car seat. She chuckled suddenly and Dante looked round, smiling.

'What amuses you, *cara*?'

'Your car looks faintly ridiculous with a child's seat on board.'

'It must get used to it, yes?' He had a quick conversation with Tullio, who took his leave of them, blew a kiss at Bea and hurried off.

'Where's he going?' asked Bea.

'To take a taxi back to work.'

'What does he do?' asked Rose as Dante helped her into the passenger seat.

'He works for me. He is good at the selling, too.'

'But not as good as you!'

'He soon will be. He is eager to learn. And as an advantage with the selling he is an attractive young man, yes?'

'Very attractive!' Rose turned round to smile at her daughter, who was cuddling Pinocchio. 'Are you comfortable, darling?'

Bea nodded happily.

'*Allora,*' said Dante and switched on the powerful engine, 'let us go home.'

'Not fast!' ordered Bea in alarm. 'I don't like fast.'

'Welcome to fatherhood,' murmured Rose. 'Soon she'll ask if we're there yet.'

Dante laughed and drove with care as they left

the airport. He touched Rose's hand fleetingly. 'Did you hear what she said?'

'She called you Daddy. You obviously liked that.'

'Very much. Did you tell her to say it?'

'No—her idea entirely.'

He let out a deep breath. 'I wanted to buy her many toys, but I did not.'

Rose nodded. 'You need her to like you for yourself.'

'*Esattamente*. You think she does?'

'Oh, yes. Apparently, you're much nicer than Holly's daddy.'

Dante laughed and reached out a hand to touch hers but put it back on the wheel at the look on her face. 'Do not worry, Rose. I will drive safely with such precious cargo on board.'

Judging by the speed of other traffic whizzing past them on the *Autostrada*, Rose found he meant what he said. Even so, she was relieved when they left the motorway at last to take a winding road lined in places with groups of tall cypress trees like exclamation marks which emphasised the breathtaking views of the rolling Tuscan landscape.

'Are we there yet?' came a voice from thc back. 'Pinocchio and Bear want to get out.'

'Very soon,' said Dante, smiling at Rose, and after a while turned off on a narrow road which wound up a steep hill in corkscrew curves he negotiated with care she was sure must be very different from his normal approach to his home. As if reading her mind, he slowed down to a crawl to drive through an entrance flanked by stone pillars and on through tiered gardens to park at the foot of steps leading to a terrace edged with small timeworn statues and stone urns full of flowers.

'Welcome to the Villa Castiglione,' said Dante and turned to smile at the wide-eyed child in the back seat.

Rose was as silent as her daughter as she gazed at the weathered golden stone of a lovely old house fronted by an arcaded loggia.

Dante opened the passenger door to help Rose out. 'Do you like my home?'

She nodded dumbly. 'It's beautiful, Dante.'

'Come out!' demanded an imperious voice and Dante laughed and hurried to release his daughter from her seat. But as he set her on her feet she reached her arms up to him in sudden alarm as someone emerged from the house.

Rose would have given much to do the same as a regal woman with silver-streaked dark hair came out to meet them.

'Mamma!' Dante laughed affectionately as he kissed her. 'You could not wait.'

'No, *caro.*' Maria Fortinari turned to Rose. 'Welcome to my son's home. Dante said I must wait, but I could not let you arrive with no one to greet you.'

Rose smiled shyly. 'How very kind. Thank you.'

'Will you introduce me to my granddaughter, *cara*?'

Bea had recovered from her attack of shyness. From her place of safety in Dante's arms, she eyed his mother with interest.

'This is Beatrice Grace, *signora*,' said Rose, and smiled at Bea. 'This lovely lady is your other grandmother, darling.'

'Another Gramma?' said Bea, surprised.

'No, *piccola*,' said Dante. 'This is my *mamma*, so she has an Italian name. She is your *nonna*.'

'Can you say that?' asked his mother gently.

Bea nodded. 'Course. Down, please, Daddy.'

A look of wonder crossed his mother's hand-some face as Dante set his daughter on her feet. She touched the fair curls gently and smiled down into the blue, unmistakable eyes. 'I would so much like a kiss, Beatrice.'

Rose crossed mental fingers, praying that Bea would cooperate, and let out the breath she was holding when her daughter held up her face for the kiss her grandmother placed on both cheeks.

'*Grazie*, Beatrice.'

Since her name sounded even more unfamil-iar pronounced Italian style, Bea shook her head. 'I'm Bea.'

Maria smiled lovingly. 'That is a very small name for a big girl like you!'

Wonderful, thought Rose, as Bea accepted her grandmother's hand to go inside.

'Come,' said Dante. 'Let us follow. You would like tea?'

'I would, please. What a lovely house, Dante.'

'I am glad you like it.' He looked up with a smile as a beaming woman came hurrying across the marble-floored hall to greet them. 'I inherited Sil-via with the house,' he muttered in English, and in Italian introduced Rose to the woman, who greeted her with a flood of what were obviously good wishes. But she threw up her hands in delight as she saw the child and came out with another flood of Italian, most of which seemed to consist of *bella, bella*, repeated several times.

'This is my son's house,' said Maria Fortinari, slanting a smile at Dante, 'so I must not give orders—'

'Which means I am neglecting you, Rose!' He gave his mother a kiss. 'Just for today, give your orders, Mamma, *per favore.*'

She nodded briskly. 'Rose, what do you desire most? Tea, coffee or to go to your room?'

'Both of us need a visit to a bathroom, *signora*,' said Rose gratefully, and took Bea's shiny pink bag from Dante. 'But, after a freshen-up, some tea would be wonderful.'

'I will take you up,' said Dante firmly, 'while Mamma arranges it.'

'*Subito, caro,*' said his mother, and brushed her hand over Bea's curls as she smiled warmly at Rose. 'It is very good to have you here.'

'It's good to be here, *signora*,' Rose assured her, and to her surprise found she meant it.

'Come,' said Dante. 'Do you need anything from your luggage now, *cara*?'

'No, thanks—' Rose eyed her daughter, who was beginning to fidget. 'Just get us to a bathroom, please.'

The room Dante showed them into was bright with sunshine, held a large bed and, most vital at that particular moment, an adjoining bathroom. Rose hurried Bea inside and a few minutes later mother and daughter, both clean of face and hands, emerged to find Dante pacing impatiently.

'Do you like the room, Rose?' he demanded.

She liked it a lot now she had time to look at the carved furniture and filmy white curtains moving lazily at the open windows. 'It's lovely.'

'Have I got a room, Daddy?' asked Bea.

'Of course, *carina*, but we shall look at it after we have tea with Nonna on the loggia.'

'What's a loggia?'

'The veranda outside, so you must wear your beautiful blue jacket—yes, Mummy?'

Rose nodded. 'I'll wear mine, too.' She hesitated. 'It was kind of your mother to come here to welcome us, Dante.'

'She could not wait to do so,' he assured her wryly, zipping Bea's jacket.

Maria Fortinari was waiting at a table set for tea when they went outside. 'Come sit by Nonna, *tesoro*,' she said, patting the chair beside her. 'You like orange juice?'

'Yes, please,' said Bea, remembering her manners, to her mother's relief.

Maria smiled in fond approval. 'There is English tea for you, Rose, and coffee for Dante, of course.'

Rose took the chair Dante held out for her next to his mother. 'What a heavenly garden,' she commented.

'We've got a garden, too,' Bea told her new grandmother. 'Tom helps Mummy in it.'

'Tom,' Dante explained, 'is Charlotte Vilari's father.'

'Gramma lives with him in his house,' said Bea, and began on her juice.

'She will miss you, *piccola*.' Maria turned to Rose. 'Forgive my English; it is not so good as my son's.'

'It sounds perfect to me,' Rose assured her. 'I can only claim some schoolgirl French, I'm afraid.

I wanted to learn Italian when I was younger, but I never had the time.'

'As I told you, Mamma, Rose was too busy qualifying as an accountant,' Dante reminded her. 'And when she had her degree she studied for more qualifications to run a bookkeeping business from her own home.' He met Rose's eyes. 'So that she could stay with Bea while she earned money to provide for her.'

'After such hard work, Rose, you must rest now you are here.' Maria Fortinari smiled down at Bea. 'Would you like one of the *trammezini*, Bea?'

'That is a sandwich, *carina*,' said her father. 'You like ham and cheese?'

'Yes, please.' Bea took one of the dainty sandwiches eagerly.

Rose sat sipping her tea, amazed that this was actually happening. Here she was in Italy with Dante, in his beautiful house and, strangest of all, taking tea with his mother. In the past, when she was facing up to life as a single parent, working hard to provide for her child, this scenario had never entered even the wildest of her dreams.

'Please eat, Rose,' urged Dante. 'You had nothing on the plane.'

'Thank you. The little cakes look delicious.'

'Silvia made them especially for you and your *mamma*, Bea,' said Maria.

'I make cakes with Gramma,' Bea informed her.

'*Che bello*! Your mother lives near you, Rose?' asked Maria.

'Yes. It's a wonderful arrangement for Bea and me.'

'For your mother, also, I think, yes?' She turned to Dante. 'Bea has finished. Would you take her for a little walk in the garden, *caro*?'

Bea looked at Rose in appeal. 'Can I go, Mummy?'

'Of course. Wipe your hands on your napkin first, please—mouth, too.'

Bea obeyed with alacrity then took the hand Dante held out. 'You got lots of flowers, Daddy.'

'*Allora, s*hall we go and count them?'

Maria cleared her throat as she watched her son walk off, hand in hand with his child. 'She is so sweet, Rose. *Grazie tante* for allowing Dante to share her. This is hard for you?'

'In some ways, yes,' said Rose honestly. 'Until a short time ago no one—not even my mother— knew that your son is Bea's father.'

Maria shook her elegantly coiffed head. 'So if you had not met Dante again in Firenze he would never know he has a child.'

'No.' Rose flushed painfully. 'By the time I knew I was pregnant Dante was already married.'

'My heart was heavy the day he married Elsa Marino,' said the other woman forcefully. 'Then one day my prayers were answered and she left him for that wealthy old fool, Enrico Calvi.'

'But until I met Dante again in Florence I didn't know that,' Rose said, and looked Maria Fortinari in the eye. 'It wasn't easy for me to come here, *signora*. I was afraid you'd think I was trying to trap a rich father for my child.'

Maria smiled ruefully. 'I confess I wondered. But then Dante described how you work so hard to make a good life for the little one. I think you are very brave. But now,' she added, suddenly brisk, 'what will you do? Dante says you refuse to marry him.'

Rose felt her colour rise. 'I'm used to running my own life, *signora*. And even though we have Bea as a common factor, Dante and I don't really know each other very well.'

'Yet you were drawn to him in the past, yes? Or Bea would not be here.'

Rose nodded ruefully. 'I fell madly in love with your son the moment I met him, and believed he felt the same about me. I was devastated when I found he had a fiancée, but my world really fell apart later when I found I was expecting his child.'

Maria winced. 'Did you curse him at the hour of Beatrice's birth?'

Rose shook her head sadly. 'No. I wanted him there with me so much I cried. But I still didn't say who I was crying for.'

Maria sighed. 'Your mother must feel much anger at my son, I think.'

'No, *signora*. I've made it very plain that what happened between Dante and me was mutual.'

Rose was glad to change the subject when Bea came running towards them with Dante in hot pursuit. 'Mummy, Mummy, there's a little pool!' Bea launched herself onto Rose's lap, her eyes bright with excitement.

'We shall take Mummy to see it later,' Dante promised.

'And tomorrow,' said his mother, 'you will come

to Fortino to meet the rest of the family. We will have a party, yes?'

Bea slid off Rose's lap to look hopefully at her grandmother. 'With balloons?'

'Yes, *carissima*. With balloons!' Maria laughed and kissed the pink cheeks. 'But now I must go home. *A domani*—until tomorrow.'

Once they'd waved his mother off Dante suggested they go indoors to show Bea her room.

'It's not bedtime yet!' objected Bea as they went upstairs.

He laughed. 'No, *piccola*, it is not. But we must show Pinocchio and Bear where to sleep, yes? Your room is here, between your *mamma*'s and mine.' He threw open the door and waited as Bea ran inside then stopped dead as she saw the doll propped up on the bed.

She looked up at Dante, wide-eyed. 'Whose dolly is that?'

'She is yours.' He caught Rose's eye and shrugged impenitently.

The doll had fair curls and blue eyes and wore jeans and a T-shirt. 'She's got clothes like me,' Bea crowed, picking the toy up to hug her.

'What do you say?' prompted Rose.

'Thank you, Daddy! You get kisses for presents,' she informed him as he picked her up.

'*Davvero*? Then you must kiss me twice because there is another present. Your dolly has a bag.'

Bea obliged with the kisses and wriggled to get down. 'What's in it?'

'Open it and see.'

The holdall, much to Bea's delight, was full of dolls' clothes.

'How lovely, darling,' said Rose, and smiled wryly at Dante. 'You couldn't resist, then?'

He shook his head. 'No. You disapprove?'

'How could I?' Rose smiled as Bea laid out every piece of miniature clothing on the bed, her eyes shining as she showed them to the doll. 'I'm only surprised you had the restraint to wait until now.'

'So am I.' His eyelids lowered. '*Allora*, now I know that presents are rewarded with kisses I shall buy something special for you, Rose, also.'

She shook her head, flushing. 'No need.'

'You mean,' he whispered, moving closer, 'that no gift is necessary for you to kiss me?'

Rose turned away hastily. 'What name shall we give her, Bea?'

Her daughter turned in surprise. 'Dolly, a'course.'

Dante threw back his head and laughed, then seized Bea and spun her round. 'So tell me, *piccola*, do you like your room?'

Bea nodded, giggling as he set her down. She frowned suddenly. 'Is it my room for always?'

Dante exchanged a look with Rose. 'Always,' he said emphatically.

Later that evening, Bea, tired out with all the excitement of the day, made no protest about going to bed in her new room with her growing collection of companions. Once she was asleep, Rose showered and changed into a dress in honour of her first dinner with Dante in the formal dining room, and felt glad she'd made the effort when she found he was wearing a lightweight suit. Dark curls gleaming in the light from the chandelier above a face alight with a smile at the sight of her, he took her breath away.

'You look very beautiful, Rose,' said Dante.

'Thank you.'

'Because this is a special occasion, Silvia has stayed to serve dinner.'

'She doesn't live in?' said Rose, surprised.

'She did in my grandmother's day, but after Nonna died Silvia surprised everyone by marrying a man she'd known in her youth. So now she comes here for an hour or two in the day, and then goes home to Mario.' Dante eyed her warily. 'She assured me that if we wish to go out any evening she will stay with Bea, but I did not think you would allow that.'

'No, indeed. Not,' added Rose hastily, 'that I don't think she's trustworthy, but—'

'You could not leave your child with a stranger who speaks no English.'

'Put like that, it sounds very cold, but yes, I suppose I do mean that.' She sighed. 'It was a big step for me to bring Bea here at all, Dante.'

'I know this. And now you are here, how do you feel?' The blue eyes lit with heat as they locked on hers. 'For me, it feels so natural, so right, to see you sitting here with me. As we should have done long ago if Elsa had not lied to me,' he said bitterly.

Rose held up a hand. 'Let's not talk about the past.'

He nodded. '*Va bene*. We shall discuss the future instead.'

'No, not tonight, Dante. Let's just sit here and enjoy Silvia's dinner together.'

His eyes softened. 'Does this mean you are enjoying your time here with me, Rose?'

She grinned. 'It beats an evening spent with my computer.'

Having eaten very little all day, Rose was more than ready for the soup Silvia served, and for the chicken roasted with herbs and vegetables that followed. She thanked the beaming woman when she came to clear away, and assured her, via Dante, that the meal had been delicious.

'*Grazie tante*, Silvia,' she said, smiling.

This prompted a voluble response Dante translated as great pleasure, that coffee and *biscotti* awaited them in the *salone* and Silvia wished them both good night.

Dante led Rose to a sitting room with a painted ceiling and furniture upholstered in ruby velvet. By the abundance of gilt-framed mirrors and pictures, it had obviously remained unchanged since his grandmother's day.

'How lovely, Dante. You've kept everything the same?'

He nodded as they sat down together on the sofa. 'My family says I should buy new things, express my own personality, but I preferred to wait.'

'Until you'd stopped grieving for your grandmother?' she said gently.

'No. Until you and I could make the changes together, Rose. *Perche*,' he said, his voice deepening, 'now I know I have a daughter, nothing will come between us this time.'

CHAPTER NINE

ROSE STIFFENED. 'ONLY because you're so desperate to be her father you're willing to take me as part of the deal!'

Dante stared at her angrily. 'This is not true. When I first saw you at Fabio's wedding I was entranced.' He turned her face up to his. 'It is plain you did not share my feelings.'

'Of course I did,' she said impatiently. 'I fell madly in love with you, Dante. Otherwise, the… the episode in the hotel room would never have happened.'

'The episode that changed your life. When you cried in my arms that night I meant only to comfort you, but the moment we kissed I felt such desperation to make love to you I was lost. When I was forced to leave you so suddenly I felt torn, as though I had left part of myself with you. Which I had,' he said bitterly. '*Dio*! How fate must have laughed when Elsa told me her lies.'

'Tears are something I must try to avoid in future,' Rose said darkly. 'They get me into too much trouble.'

Dante seized her hand. 'You cried the night in your house when we quarrelled, yes?'

'Yes.' She smiled brightly. 'So no more quarrelling, either.'

'This is a good plan,' he agreed. 'So now when I say we must marry you will not argue?'

If he made it clear he loved her for herself, rather than part of the deal that gained him a daughter, there would be no argument at all. He made it crystal clear he wanted her physically, but she would have to be convinced that his heart was involved, too, before she agreed to anything permanent between them. And if that was asking for the moon, so be it. She'd managed without him in her life before and she would do it again rather than enter into a relationship where her feelings were greater than his.

'I still think we should take more time to get to know each other first.'

'Gran Dio!' Dante thrust his free hand through his hair. 'How much time do you need? We have

wasted too many years already.' He released her hand and sprang up. *'Scusi!'*

Rose watched, dismayed, as he strode from the room. Did he intend on coming back? But, to her relief, Dante returned quickly, holding out a leather-bound diary.

'Open it,' he ordered.

Her eyes widened as she saw it was dated the year they'd met. As she took it from him, a withered rosebud slid out.

'It fell from your hair at the wedding,' Dante informed her curtly. 'I have kept it all this time, like a sentimental fool.'

She felt her throat thicken and blinked furiously as she carefully replaced the pressed bud. 'I must check on Bea,' she said, getting up, but Dante barred her way.

'I have just done so. She is sleeping peacefully.' He took her hand and drew her down on the sofa beside him. 'You say we do not know each other well enough to marry yet, but the best way for this is to live together, the three of us as a family.'

She looked at him squarely. 'And there's the buzz word. Without Bea in the picture, would you be in such a hurry?'

Dante dropped her hand and moved away, his face drawn. 'What more can I do to convince you? I even embarrass myself by showing you the rose I kept. You say you fell in love with me at first sight, but now your feelings for me are very different, yes?' He shrugged. '*Non importa*. For Bea's sake, we shall marry, and soon. My child shall not grow up believing I do not want her.'

'But what shall I *do* here?' she said unsteadily. 'You're away a lot. At home I have my work—'

'You could work here also if you wish. Harriet helps Leo a great deal. She is very good at taking visitors around Fortino.'

'She speaks Italian?'

'Yes. She taught it at one time. French also.'

Her face fell. 'I don't do any of that. My sole talent is with figures.'

'You could help Harriet by taking over the English-speaking tourists.' Dante turned to look at her, his eyes bleak. 'Also, I will travel less after we marry.'

Will, Rose noted, not *would*. She had known all along that saying yes to the trip was saying yes to marrying Dante. Which was all she'd ever wanted from the first moment she'd met him; even more so now he'd matured into a man who'd suffered enough, courtesy of Elsa. And so had she. For Bea's sake, if nothing else, it was time to move on. Grow up at last. And surely, once they were married, she could make Dante love her for herself, not just as his child's mother. But what, said an inner voice, if he never does?

'I'll think about it,' she said at last.

Dante eyed her suspiciously. 'What are you saying?'

'I can't just walk away from my life at a moment's notice, Dante. I'd have to sell my business first, for one thing. So you'll have to give me more time.'

He shook his head in wonder. '*Dio*, that is not the answer I wanted, Rose.'

'Take it or leave it,' she said, shrugging, then quailed inwardly at the sudden fire in his eyes.

'I will take it! I will also take this,' he added huskily and kissed her with sudden fierce demand that shook her to her toes. He pulled her onto his lap, his lips and hands caressing her into a response which swept through her with such heat he pulled her to her feet and led her up the stairs to the gallery. At the open door of Bea's room, they gazed at their sleeping child for a moment then Dante took away what breath Rose had left by picking her up to carry her along the gallery to his room. He laid her on his bed and began taking off his clothes. She shot upright in protest.

'Wait a minute!'

He shot her an imperious look. 'No. I have waited long enough.' He knelt on the bed beside her and began undressing her. 'You may not love me, but you want me. Do you deny it?'

'No, I don't.' She took in a deep breath. 'But don't do this in anger, Dante.'

His eyes smouldered as he slid the dress from her shoulders. 'No, *bella*, not in anger.' He took down the hair she'd spent so much time over earlier and buried his face in it. 'I want you, Rose.' He removed the last of her clothes and held her shivering body against his hard male nakedness with a growl of pure male satisfaction. 'Tonight,' he said huskily, 'we finish what we began so many years ago, yes?'

'You've made love to me since then,' she said unsteadily as his lips moved down her throat.

He kissed the pulse he found throbbing there.

'But once again only in haste. Tonight I will show you what loving can be for us, *tesoro*.'

Rose felt his heart thudding against hers and looked up into the brilliant eyes moving over her in open possession. *Yes*, she thought fiercely. *Show me. I want this.* 'You'll have to make allowances, Dante,' she said unevenly, her breath catching as he slid his lips down her throat.

'For what, *amore*?' he whispered.

'You've obviously done this a lot and I…well, I haven't. As you know, I had a boyfriend in college, but there's been no one since Bea was born.'

Dante held her closer. 'And was he a skilled lover, this college boyfriend?'

'No, he was much better at playing rugby,' she said unevenly. 'But I was fond of him and he made me laugh.'

'It is good to laugh together,' agreed Dante, and kissed her with mounting urgency. 'We shall laugh together many times, I hope, but at this moment, *tesoro*, I want you in all the ways a man wants a woman.'

Rose fully expected an onslaught as he sought instant relief for the tension she could feel building in his body, but instead Dante took infinite pleasure in kissing and caressing every inch of her with clever, inciting hands that tuned her entire body to such a pitch of longing she gave a hoarse little cry of protest as he paused an instant to use protection then took her mouth in a devouring kiss as his body fused with hers in a jolt of such pure sensation she fought for breath, her heart hammering against his. She lay relishing the almost painful pleasure of it for an instant before he withdrew slightly then thrust again to what felt like the very heart of her, his eyes like blue fires burning down into hers as he began showing her exactly what the art of loving should be. He kissed her as he made love to her, the rhythm slow at first until he felt her desire mount to match his, but at last he took her hard and fast towards the culmination that finally overwhelmed them both and, with a smothered cry, she came apart in his arms, and he surrendered to his own release.

Dante drew the covers over them and turned her in his arms to hold her close. 'Rose,' he whispered later, 'I do not wish to move, but soon I must take you back to the guest room. Bea might come looking for you and find the bed empty.'

She nodded, flushing. 'You're right.'

'Tomorrow,' said Dante with emphasis, 'we bring your clothes to my room and tell our daughter you will be sharing it with me.'

Rose braced herself as she shook her head. 'I'd rather not do that until things are more settled between us, Dante.'

'Ah!' His face darkened. 'This is my punishment, Rose?'

'Punishment?'

'For my sins,' he said bitterly. 'I did not tell you about Elsa, I left you with child—'

'Since the child is the light of my life, I wouldn't punish you for that, Dante.' She looked at him in appeal. 'I just want you to slow down a little, to give me more time to get used to—'

'To me?' he said quickly. 'Yet, here in my arms, I thought I made you happy, Rose.'

'You know you did,' she said, flushing, and turned her head way. 'That part of our relationship would obviously be good.'

'All of it will be good,' he said with passion. 'But if you want me to wait until you are also sure of this I will do so.' He gave a mirthless laugh. 'I am good at the waiting. I have been waiting for you for years, Rose.'

She turned on him sharply, her eyes flashing. 'If that's true, why didn't you come looking for me once you were free?'

His chin lifted. 'Charlotte told me you had someone else in your life. She would not say who it was, so I believed, *naturalmente*, that it was a man.' He shook his head in wonder. 'While all the time it was the daughter I did not know I possessed.'

'I begged Charlotte to keep my baby secret. So she did.'

'You were ashamed of Bea?'

She glared at him. 'No, I was not! I was merely afraid that if any of your friends saw you anywhere near my child they would know exactly who her father was. And because you were married, it would have been disaster all round.'

'But Bea resembles you, not me,' said Dante, surprised.

'Not the smile and those eyes of yours. They're a dead giveaway. My mother took one look at you two together and knew straight away.'

'*Va bene*, now the whole world will know,' he said with satisfaction, and slid out of bed. 'No. Stay there, *cara*. I have a present for you.' He licked his lips as he leaned over her. 'So I will get kisses, yes?'

Rose laughed. 'Very probably!'

'I have dreamed of this so often, yet now you are really here at last. Where you belong, yes?' Dante gave her a look that curled her toes then turned away to open a drawer and took out a small box before sliding back into bed.

'You don't have to give me presents to get a kiss,' she remarked, eyeing the box.

'Then I will kiss you first,' he said and did so with such lingering pleasure that Rose kissed him back in kind and melted against him, breathing in the scent of his skin as he nuzzled his lips against her neck. 'Open the box, *tesoro*,' he whispered.

Rose obeyed, and breathed in sharply at the sight of a gold ring set with a baguette emerald between two rose-cut diamonds. 'Oh, Dante,' she breathed, tears welling in her eyes.

He sat upright, pulling her up with him. 'You do not like it?'

'Of *course* I like it,' she said hoarsely, and knuckled the tears from her eyes. 'It's just that I can't accept it just yet.'

'Why not?' he demanded, eyes suddenly cold.

She eyed him in appeal. 'Don't look at me like that! I'm just asking you to wait a little longer.'

Dante closed the ring box with a snap and tossed it on the bedside table. *'Va bene,'* he said shortly. 'But I will wait only until I take you back to England. Tomorrow, you will have a taste of what life could be for us here in Fortino. After that, if you still say no to me it will be the last time. It is against my nature to beg and I will do so no more—but then I will make legal arrangements to share our daughter.'

Rose stared at him in horror. 'Dante, listen—'

'No, Rose. It is you who must listen. It is best we are clear on this. Say yes and we live a normal married life. If not, you know what will happen. *Allora,*' he added silkily, 'since I have you here and now in my bed, I will enjoy the privilege while I can.' And he pulled her closer and made love to her all over again. But in the throes of the climax that engulfed her she waited in vain for the words which would have ended all argument, whichever language he chose. *'Ti amo'* was one bit of Italian she would have understood perfectly well.

CHAPTER TEN

ROSE WOKE TO bright sunshine and found her daughter at the foot of the guest room bed with Dante, shaking her head at her mother in disapproval.

'Up, Mummy. Party time.'

'Not yet, *piccola*,' said Dante, laughing. 'First we have breakfast. So let us leave Mummy to her bath and you and I shall walk in the garden until she is ready.'

Rose blinked in surprise at her daughter, who was wearing fresh jeans and T-shirt, her face shining and curls brushed. 'Good morning, darling. Did you get dressed all by yourself?'

Bea beamed up at Dante. 'Daddy helped me. But I washed and did teeth by myself.'

Rose eyed Dante with unwilling respect. He was diving into the deep end of fatherhood with enthusiasm. 'Then I'd better get a move on and do mine, hadn't I?'

'You are tired, *cara*?' said Dante softly, his eyes gleaming.

'Travelling always affects me that way,' she said, and thrust her hair back from her flushed face. 'Now, give me ten minutes and I'll join you for breakfast—I'm hungry.'

After a swift shower, Rose wrapped her wet hair in a towel to style later, slapped on some moisturiser and pulled on jeans and sweater. Something more elegant could be achieved later on before they left for Fortino. She felt a pang of apprehension again at the thought of meeting the rest of Dante's family. But his mother had been kind and Rose already knew Harriet, so she would have support from a fellow Brit among the alien corn. As she hurried downstairs she could hear Bea chattering away to Dante as they came in from the garden and felt a shamed little pang of jealousy of the man who was making her little girl so happy.

Silvia came hurrying through the hall with a tray as Rose went down, and smiled and wished her good morning, but in a different accent from Dante's.

'*Buongiorno,*' echoed Rose, hoping it sounded

right, and received such a beaming smile in response assumed it did.

'There you are,' said Dante, getting up as she went outside on the loggia. 'Are you dressed warmly enough to eat outside?'

'I asked Daddy if we could,' said Bea.

'And Daddy said yes, of course,' said Rose, smiling.

He shrugged, grinning. *'Naturalmente.'* He pulled out a chair for her.

'That means a'course,' Bea told her, and smiled at Silvia as the woman poured orange juice into her glass. *'Grazie,'* she said proudly, in exact imitation of Dante. 'Was that right, Daddy?'

'Perfect.' He nodded in agreement as Silvia, smiling fondly at the child, spoke rapidly to him. 'Silvia says you are a clever girl.'

Eating a leisurely breakfast outside in the cool sunlit morning was such a contrast to the normal routine in the Palmer household. Rose suppressed all uneasy thoughts of Dante's threat the night before and smiled as she described their usual morning chaos. 'It takes more effort some days than others, but I always manage to get Bea to nursery school on time.'

'Do you like school, Bea?' Dante asked.

She nodded. 'The teacher reads stories. And we do painting and make things.'

'Did you tell her you were coming to Italy for a holiday?'

'Yes. To Daddy's house.'

Rose eyed her daughter wryly. 'And what did she say?'

'What a lucky girl! Can I get down now?'

By the time Rose had washed her daughter's face and hands and collected Dolly, Pinocchio and Bear, Silvia had brewed a fresh pot of coffee, so Rose sat down to share it with Dante while Bea played with her toys on the steps beside them.

'Sorry about the face and hair,' murmured Rose. 'I'll do something better before we go.'

'I like to see you like this.' He shrugged. 'Elsa drank only black coffee in the morning and refused to leave her room until her face and coiffure were perfect.'

'Who's Elsa?' asked Bea.

Dante shot a remorseful glance at Rose. 'A lady I used to know.'

'Will she be at the party?'

'No, *piccola*. Today is for family only.'

Bea scrambled to her feet. 'Mummy, can I have more juice?'

'Go to the kitchen to ask Silvia for some,' suggested Rose. 'Daddy will tell you what to say.'

'I can get it,' said Dante instantly, but Rose shook her head.

'It's a good way to learn the language.'

He bent down to Bea. 'You must say "*Succo, per favore,* Silvia".'

She repeated it solemnly then went running into the house.

'Forgive me, Rose,' said Dante heavily. 'I did not think. I will not mention Elsa again.'

She shook her head. 'It doesn't matter.'

His eyes flared as he pulled her out of her chair. 'It does matter. Now you and Bea are in my life, I wish to forget she ever existed,' he said, and kissed her fiercely.

But without Bea this would not be happening, Rose thought unhappily, and with iron will managed to keep from melting into his embrace as he crushed her to him.

Dante released her, smiling as Rose picked up the towel she'd lost in the encounter.

She thrust her hair back from her hot face.

'Maybe you should see how Bea is getting along with Silvia.'

'With pleasure!' He went into the house and eventually returned with a plastic beaker of juice, his daughter running beside him.

'This is a special mug for me, Mummy,' she informed Rose, beaming. 'And I said *grazie* to Silvia for the juice.'

'You're a star! Come and sit down by Dolly to drink. Only don't spill anything on her.'

Bea obeyed carefully. 'Mummy, can I wear my party dress today?'

'I've been meaning to ask about that,' said Rose. 'What do you want us to wear today, Dante?'

'My women will look ravishing whatever they wear,' he assured her.

'Only if they're wearing something appropriate and don't feel out of place,' Rose said tartly. 'So are you wearing a suit?'

'No, *cara*. Just ordinary clothes and one of my leather jackets.'

'None of your clothes look very ordinary, Dante.'

'Mummy!' repeated Bea imperiously. 'Can I wear my dress?'

'Yes,' said Rose in sudden decision. 'I'll wear a dress, too. But we'll take some jeans and a T-shirt for you, just in case. What time are we due at Fortino, Dante?'

'Noon.'

'In that case I'd better make a start on my hair. You can take a look at the clothes I've brought, Dante, and choose for me.'

'I always do that, Mummy,' said Bea, pouting.

'We shall choose together,' said her father hastily, and snatched her up to give her a piggyback up the stairs.

On the approach to Dante's childhood home through the vast vineyards of Fortino, the house which came into view looked familiar to Rose.

'It's the label on your Fortinari Classico,' she said, impressed. 'I'd assumed it was a reproduction of some Renaissance villa.' She bit her lip. 'It's very grand, Dante.'

'But in bad condition when my parents inherited it,' he informed her. 'Much work was necessary to make it look as it does today. Part of it is used as offices, so Mamma wants a smaller, more private place to enjoy my father's retirement. She would like Leo and Harriet to take over Fortino.'

'Will they do that?'

'Harriet says Leo spends most of his time here anyway, so she is willing to make the change. But Leo is attached to his present house because it is the home he brought Harriet to as a bride.'

'Look, balloons, Daddy!' piped up a voice from the back. 'And lots of people.'

Bea was right. As Dante parked the car, people came streaming out of the house onto a loggia far bigger and grander than the one at the Villa Castiglione, with brightly coloured balloons tied to its venerable pillars.

'Do I look all right?' demanded Rose urgently, and Dante picked up her hand and squeezed it.

'You are perfect,' he said, and got out to help his little family from the car.

Maria Fortinari came hurrying down the steps to greet them and kissed Rose in warm welcome, then planted kisses on her granddaughter's cheeks. 'You both look so beautiful,' she exclaimed, and turned to the distinguished silver-haired man following behind. 'Our newest granddaughter, *caro*.' She drew Rose forward. 'And this is Rose, her *mamma*.'

Lorenzo Fortinari took Rose by the shoulders and kissed her on both cheeks. '*Benvenuti*, Rose.' He smiled down at the child clinging to Dante's hand. 'Welcome to you, also, *piccola*. May I have a kiss?'

'This is *my* daddy, Bea,' Dante informed his daughter. 'But to you he is *Nonno*.'

Much to Rose's relief, Bea held up her face for her grandfather's kiss, then her eyes lit up and she broke away to dart up the steps to the people clustered there watching. 'Auntie Charlotte, Auntie Charlotte!'

'Honey Bea!' Charlotte Vilari hugged her tightly. 'How's my lovely girl?'

Bea smiled up at her joyfully. 'I got a big secret, Auntie.'

'Have you, darling?'

Bea nodded vigorously. 'Dante's my daddy!'

There was delighted laughter and, to Rose's surprise, a ripple of applause from the people gathered waiting there. Charlotte passed Bea to her husband, Fabio, and hurried down the steps to throw her arms round her friend, both of them too emotional to say a word until Rose drew back, grinning happily through her tears.

'This is a lovely surprise—mind the bump, little mother!'

Dante gave them time to recover then introduced Rose to his sister Mirella and her husband, Franco. 'This is Rose,' he said with pride. 'And the little angel with Signora Vilari is my daughter—as she has already informed you.'

'And I am his brother,' said a deep voice with a more pronounced accent, and Dante grinned as he turned Rose to meet Leo Fortinari, easily recognisable as an older, more saturnine version of his brother.

'*Il capo*, Rose. My boss,' said Dante, saluting smartly.

'Senior partner, not boss,' said a familiar voice as Harriet Fortinari detached Rose from Dante. 'I'm so glad to see you here. Come and meet my children—they are dying to play with Bea. Will she like that?'

'She'll love it,' Rose assured her, and looked at Dante. 'Will you get her?'

'Yes, *amore*.' He grinned. 'If you think Charlotte will let her go.'

Leo Fortinari issued strict instructions to his son, Luca, and daughter, Chiara, to take great care of Bea, and Franco Paglia did the same with Mario, Renzo and Vittoria, who were older, but just as eager to play with the child as the others, but brought her running back to Rose first.

'I want my jeans,' Bea said urgently, and Maria Fortinari nodded in approval.

'Come with me and your *mamma* to change, *bella*. It would not be good to spoil that lovely dress.'

While the exchange was made, Maria smiled warmly at Rose and patted her cheek. 'Welcome to our home, *cara*.'

Rose blinked hard. 'Thank you, *signora*.'

The striking dark eyes misted over. 'It is so good to see Dante happy again. I am very grateful to you.'

'Nonna!' said Bea, dancing impatiently in her blue trainers. 'Want to play now—please,' she added at a look from her mother.

'*Va bene*,' said Maria, clearing her throat. 'Let us go out. Come, Rose, join the others for a glass of wine while I return to the kitchen.'

'Can I help in any way?'

Maria patted her hand. 'Not today, *grazie*. I have help in the kitchen. Enjoy the day with the others.'

Rose found it only too easy to enjoy herself in company with Charlotte, Harriet and Mirella on the loggia while she watched a very happy, excited Bea running riot with the other children.

'I'm on lemonade,' said Charlotte, pulling a face as she raised her glass to her husband, who was talking to the other men, but with one eye on his wife.

'It is best for now,' said Mariella with sympathy.

'You still have to keep off the wine if you nurse the baby yourself,' put in Harriet. 'But it's worth it, isn't it, Rose?'

Rose smiled ruefully as she watched Bea trying to catch a ball Luca tossed to her. 'I couldn't do it. I had to resort to bottles.'

'I remember how upset you were about it,' said Charlotte. 'She tried so hard to be the perfect mother,' she told the others.

'You succeeded,' said Harriet, waving a hand towards Bea. 'Just look at the result—oops, she's fallen over.'

Rose surged to her feet but Dante was first to scoop up his daughter and make anxious enquiries.

'Down, Daddy,' she said crossly. 'Want to play!'

Dante obeyed, and exchanged a wry grin with Rose as Bea returned to the ball game. 'It is hard to stand back, yes?'

'Unless they're bleeding you leave them to it,' Harriet advised, and Mirella laughed.

'It took me a long time to learn that.'

'Are you taking notes, Charlotte?' asked Rose.

Her friend smiled contentedly. 'I'm just enjoying the moment, love. To have you and Bea here like this is just wonderful.'

'Mamma thinks so, too,' said Mirella. 'She has worried much over Dante, but now he is happy, Mamma is happy. I am happy, too,' she added, sniffing hard.

'So when are you going to marry him, Rose?' asked Charlotte bluntly.

'There's a lot to consider before making any decisions. For one thing, I have to sell my business first.' And far more vital than that, before she said yes she needed to be sure that Dante wanted her as his wife rather than just the mother of his child.

'Just put it in the hands of an agent—the house, too.'

'First I need to talk with my mother—and your

father, too.' Rose grinned suddenly. 'I was most impressed with *your* mother, Mirella. She didn't turn a hair when Bea told her my mother lives with Tom in his house.'

Mirella laughed. 'She was so delighted her new granddaughter was talking to her, yes?'

Rose nodded. 'Though to be fair to Charlotte's father, he'd marry my mother tomorrow.'

'Perhaps Grace will finally agree if you marry Dante,' said Charlotte.

'Not "if", Charlotte, "when",' said Dante, coming to join them. 'For me it could be tomorrow, but Rose is making me wait.'

'What for, Rose?' demanded her friend as Mirella and Harriet rushed to settle a squabble among their offspring.

Charlotte's question was hard to answer. Here in Fortino, surrounded by Dante's warm, hospitable family, Rose experienced an urgent longing to become part of it. Grace would understand; it was what she'd always wanted for her girls. 'We've only just got together again,' she said lightly. 'Give me time to get used to the idea. I've been running my own life—and Bea's—for quite a time, remember.'

'But there's a man here who will gladly help you with that if you let him,' Charlotte said. 'Right, Dante?'

'With great pleasure,' he agreed, and smiled fondly as he watched Bea playing with the other children. 'She is a delight. I still find it hard to believe I am her father—'

'You have doubts?' demanded Rose.

'None!' He grasped her hand tightly. 'It is you who have the doubts, not I, Rose. I long to marry you and give you and Bea the life you both deserve. We would be good together,' he added, his eyes boring into hers to remind her how it had been between them the night before.

'So for heaven's sake say yes, Rose,' said Charlotte and smiled up at Fabio. 'If Rose and Dante get married in England you'll just have to let me fly there, darling.'

Fabio flung out a hand to Dante in appeal. 'In that case, *amico*, make it soon, yes?'

'I will do my best,' Dante promised, and sprang to attention as his mother came out on the loggia. 'It is time to eat, Mamma?'

'*Subito, figlio mio.*' She smiled at Rose. 'I have

washed the little one's face and hands with all the others. So now we eat, yes?'

A long table had been set up in the garden with a snowy-white cloth obscured by great platters of food and soon everyone was crowded round it, elbow to elbow, and talking non-stop. The children were seated together at one end, with a parent occasionally jumping up to serve them or settle squabbles. Vittoria and Chiara vied with each other to look after Bea, who was so obviously having the time of her life Rose eventually relaxed, enjoying not only the meal but the feeling of belonging.

Lorenzo Fortinari got up when the wine was poured and held his glass high. 'A toast to welcome Rose and little Bea to Fortino!'

Everyone surged to their feet to echo the toast, and Rose followed suit, smiling gratefully. 'From Bea and myself, *grazie tante*!'

'Brava, carissima,' said Dante as she sat down amidst cheers.

She smiled. 'Just look at Bea. She's having so much fun.'

He nodded. 'It is easy to see her gold head among her Italian cousins.'

Mirella leaned forward, rolling her eyes. 'Vittoria will want to dye her hair blond now.'

Harriet groaned. 'And Chiara—maybe the boys, too!'

Franco shuddered theatrically. 'Do not even think of it, *per favore*!'

At the burst of laughter which greeted this Maria Fortinari came to join them to make sure Rose was enjoying herself and to press her to eat more food.

Rose smiled warmly. '*Signora*, I couldn't eat another thing, thank you. It was such a delicious meal.'

'I did not make all of it, *cara*. Letizia, my cook, is still with me, *grazie a Dio*.'

'Ah, but you made the *pollo Parmigiano*, Mamma,' said Dante, and kissed his fingers. 'It was superb, as always.'

'I make it with the identical recipe.' Harriet sighed. 'But it's never the same.'

Leo patted her hand. 'It is good enough for me. And you baked the wonderful English apple pies for us today, *amore*.'

'Much too wonderful,' said Charlotte, patting her stomach. 'I was greedy.'

'It is only natural right now,' said Fabio fondly.

At one time Rose would have been painfully envious as she watched the other couples together, but now that she had the chance of Dante permanently in her life, envy could be a thing of the past. Whatever his feelings for her, perhaps it was time to grasp this opportunity with both hands and make their marriage work for Bea's sake. And for her own, she admitted, her eyes on Dante.

'Just look at him,' murmured Charlotte as he went off to check on his daughter. 'He's besotted with her.'

Mirella watched her brother laughing among the group of clamouring children. 'He is such good uncle, but now he can be wonderful father at last.' She smiled ruefully at Rose. 'My English is not like Dante's.'

'But very good, just the same,' said Rose huskily. 'I must try to learn Italian as quickly as I can.'

'My wife can give you lessons,' suggested Leo Fortinari to her surprise.

'Brilliant idea, darling!' Harriet smiled at Rose. 'Don't worry; I'm a qualified teacher—and you'll be a much easier prospect than a classroom of teenage girls.'

* * *

'You have enjoyed the day?' asked Dante on the drive back. 'It was so good to watch you eating and laughing with my family—and with Charlotte. I did not tell you she would be there. I wished to give you a happy surprise.'

'Which you certainly did. Thank you. It was good to see a familiar face, though heaven knows your family's welcome couldn't have been warmer.'

'I am glad you were pleased. Our little one played very happily with her cousins, yes?'

'Bea had such a great time,' Rose assured him, and laughed softly as she glanced over into the back seat. 'She's fast asleep, but still clutching the string of her balloon.'

'It is a pity we must wake her to put her to bed.' He shot her a commanding look. 'I am impatient to have you both with me permanently.'

She nodded. 'I know, Dante.' She hesitated, but couldn't quite make herself take the plunge. 'Thank you for being patient with me.'

'Then I am a good actor.' He turned smouldering eyes on her. 'Inside, I am not patient at all. Sleep with me tonight, Rose.' He touched a slim warm hand to her knee. 'If not your husband yet, you want me as a lover, yes?'

Not much point in denying it. Rose nodded silently.

Dante let out a deep, unsteady breath. 'Then tonight we'll make up for all the nights after you leave me alone.'

Why not? thought Rose. If making love with her would make Dante miss her all the more she was all for it. And for her it would make up for the times she'd cried herself to sleep over him in the past. Besides, she wanted him physically in a way she would never experience with any other man, so why fight it?

The silence between them was thick with sensual tension as Dante carried his daughter into his house. Bea never stirred as Rose sponged her face and hands and put her in her pyjamas, nor when Dante laid her gently in her bed and kissed the sleeping face. Then he led Rose outside onto the gallery and seized her in his arms.

'Now I take you to my bed,' he said huskily.

'I should shower—' she began, but he shook his head and picked her up.

'We shower together—afterwards.'

To Rose it seemed so natural, so right to slide naked into Dante's arms in bed she almost said yes then and there to the prospect of doing so for the rest of her life as he rubbed his cheek against hers.

'*This* is where you are meant to be,' he said as though reading her mind. His arms tightened. 'Where you should have been all these years.'

She had no desire to resurrect the past. 'I'm here now, so do we talk or did you have something else in mind?'

Dante's laugh was so joyous that Rose laughed with him as his lips and hands told her exactly what he had in mind as he made love to her with patience which ended abruptly when for the first time she initiated some caresses of her own. Dante surrendered joyously to his hunger and took her to the very peak of physical rapture and held her there, gasping with her in the throes of it before they returned to earth.

'If we get married—' she said later, lying bone-less in Dante's arms.

'*When* we get married,' Dante corrected and

turned her face up to his. 'What were you going to say, *amore*?'

'I wondered what kind of wedding you had with Elsa.' So they could do something completely different—if her answer was yes. As it was going to be, she realised. There was no way she could deprive her child of the kind of life she'd experienced today.

'Elsa was in such a hurry after I told her about you she changed her plans for the wedding of the year into a brief visit to the town hall—but with many photographers there to record the wedding of Elsa Marino, supermodel, *naturalmente*.' Dante shrugged. 'I was glad of a civil ceremony. It was easier to end our marriage later when she met Enrico and his money.'

'But you must have been in love with her in the beginning, surely?'

'I was attracted by the outer beautiful shell— also she was very skilled in bed,' he said bluntly. 'We knew each other for so short a time I did not discover the true Elsa until our wedding night, when she told me the pregnancy was a lie, and that she had no intention of having children ever.'

'What on earth did you do?' said Rose.

He took a deep breath. 'For the first time in my life I could have done violence to a woman. To avoid this I did something which injured her far more. I went into the *salone* of our suite and locked the door. She screamed and cursed me for rejecting her but, as I told you before, and I swear it is the truth, I never touched her again throughout the sham of our marriage.' Dante shuddered and hugged her close. 'No more talk of Elsa, *per favore.*'

Rose agreed fervently. 'I just asked so we could plan something completely different for *our* wedding.' She felt the graceful, muscular body tense against hers as she turned her face up to his.

'*Finalmente*! You will marry me?'

'You said it's what you want.'

His eyes blazed with triumph. 'More than anything in my life.' He caught her close and kissed her passionately. 'I promise you will never regret this, Rose.'

'I'll hold you to that.' She kissed him back.

Dante rubbed his cheek against hers. 'Now you have said yes at last we must make plans. We could have the wedding at the Hermitage. Tony does these often. Then after the ceremony we have a party like the Vilari wedding.' He reached out a hand to switch on the bedside lamp and looked down into Rose's face. 'But this time you will be the bride and I shall gain my heart's desire of a child at last.'

Tears welled in her eyes, and Dante caught her to him. 'Do not cry, *tesoro*. If you do not like this idea—'

'Oh, but I do, I do—I love it,' she said thickly, and knuckled away the tears which had welled at the mention of a child. Not, she assured herself, ashamed, that she was jealous of Bea. She just wanted Dante's heart's desire to include her as well as Bea.

Dante slid out of bed to take a handkerchief from his dressing chest and dried her eyes. 'What can I do to dry your tears?'

Rose sniffed inelegantly. 'Just hold me, please.'

'Always,' he said, and slid under the covers to pull her close. 'So why did you weep, *cara*?'

'Because it's exactly the kind of wedding I wanted but didn't like to ask.'

'Perche?' he said, mystified. 'Rose, surely you

must know by now that I would give you and Bea the moon if I could.'

'How lovely,' she said unsteadily and grinned at him. 'But a Hermitage wedding with our families around us is all I want—complete with our own personal bridesmaid!'

Dante laughed and held her closer. 'Bea will enjoy that very much, I think.'

'She will,' said Rose fervently, and then frowned. 'Will your mother mind having the wedding in England?'

'No, because she is so delighted that I am marrying again. And to please her—and myself—we can repeat our vows privately later before a priest in Fortino. But we must arrange our wedding very soon, not only because I am impatient, but so Charlotte can be there.' Dante gave a deep sigh of satisfaction. 'I am sure Tony will be happy to make space in his Hermitage schedule for his favourite cousin.'

Rose smiled at him ruefully. 'I can't believe this is all happening. Pinch me, Dante, so I know I'm not dreaming.' She hissed as he gently pinched a nipple. 'I didn't mean there! You'll have to kiss it better now.'

'If you insist.' He sighed and then eyed her sternly as she punched his shoulder. 'Be still while I obey your command.'

CHAPTER ELEVEN

THE REST OF their stay at the Villa passed so quickly in visits to Dante's parents to ask their blessing, and to Harriet and Leo and the Vilaris to give their news, the day of departure was on them all too soon.

'It seems a shame to drag you all the way to England just to take us home,' said Rose the night before.

Dante shook his head. 'I must make sure you arrive safely, then I will stay the night in your bed and try not to think of all the nights when I'll lie in this bed alone until you come back to me.'

'You spent a lot of nights in it alone in the past,' she pointed out.

'But that was before I knew the joy of sharing it with you, *amore*. Now it will be hard to sleep without you.'

'You haven't slept much *with* me!'

'*Certo*. Why waste time in sleep when we can

make love?' Dante held her close. 'But it is not
just the lovemaking I will miss. It is having you
here to talk and laugh with, to share my life with
you and Bea.' He tensed as he heard a cry from
his daughter's room and shrugged on his dressing
gown. 'Stay there, *amore*. I will fetch her.'

'You're in Daddy's bed,' Bea accused tearfully
when Dante brought her to Rose.

'Mummy's going to sleep here with me now,'
he informed his daughter.

'When I get bad dreams I sleep in Mummy's
bed,' she told him militantly.

Dante laid her down alongside Rose and got
in beside them. 'But now I will be there, too, to
chase the bad dreams away,' he said firmly and
smiled at Rose as their child nodded contentedly
and laid her curly head on his shoulder.

With the prospect of parting from Dante loom-
ing over her, Rose found it hard to smile for Bea
on the flight home as her child chattered about
seeing Gramma and Tom again. She felt uneasy
and oddly tearful. Stupid, she lectured herself.
Soon they would be married and could be together
for the rest of their lives. A prospect she'd never

imagined, ever. And in the meantime she would have enough to occupy her with her normal workload added to the wedding arrangements and finding a purchaser for her business.

'You are sad, *tesoro*?' said Dante quietly as the plane began its descent into Heathrow.

'Yes,' she said honestly and tried to smile.

He clasped her hand tightly. 'I will miss you both so much,' he said as Bea began to stir from her nap. 'Wake up, *piccola*. We are almost there.'

Since Rose had texted her mother on the car journey from the airport, Grace and Tom were waiting at the front door of Willow House, arms outstretched as Bea ran to them, talking at the top of her voice.

'Gramma,' she cried as Grace snatched her close to kiss her, 'Daddy's mummy is *Nonna*, and his daddy is *Nonno*, and I got lots of cousins, and Daddy bought me a doll. Her name is Dolly.' She turned to Tom, arms up. 'Auntie Charlotte gave me a present for you, Tom.' Beaming, she gave him two smacking kisses as he swung her up.

'Thank you, Honey Bea,' he said, returning the kisses with gusto as Rose hugged her mother. 'How was Auntie Charlotte?'

'She's a lot fatter,' Bea informed him as he put her down. She ran to Rose and picked up her left hand. 'Look, Gramma—Daddy gave Mummy a present.'

Grace took a look at the ring and hugged Rose close again. 'How absolutely lovely.' She smiled warmly at Dante as he brought the luggage. 'Welcome back.'

'Thank you, *signora*.' He kissed her hand and turned to Tom. 'Charlotte is looking very well, sir.'

'Good to know. Any hope of Fabio letting her fly over soon?' said Tom wryly.

'As a matter of fact, yes,' said Rose, and exchanged a smiling glance with Dante. 'Let's go inside so we can tell you why.'

Bea was incensed the next day when she found Dante was leaving, and clung to him in tears when the taxi arrived.

'Soon,' Dante promised as he held his child in his arms, 'we shall be together at the Villa Castiglione, but until then you must help Mummy and Gramma plan the wedding, yes?'

Bea's tears dried a little as she looked at her mother. 'Can I, Mummy?'

Rose nodded. 'Of course, as soon as Daddy arranges the date for the party.'

Bea brightened. 'With balloons?'

Dante laughed as he set her on her feet. 'With balloons, yes! Now I must go, but first I will kiss your *mamma* goodbye.' He held Rose close as he kissed her. 'Do not work too hard, and take great care of yourself, *carina*.'

'You, too,' she said and smiled brightly.

The period that followed was one of the most hectic of Rose's life, but the soonest wedding date possible for everyone concerned was a month later, which made it still possible for Charlotte to come, but did not please Dante. 'Tony Mostyn could not do it sooner, even for me! But this is good for you, Rose?'

'Yes. It's not long. Actually, I'm glad of time to get everything settled.' Secretly, she would have preferred it sooner, with less time to worry about Dante's motives for marrying her. But every time doubts crept in she thought of Bea, and how she had clung to her daddy as they parted. And as

Rose had done since her child was born, she did what was best for Bea, which in this case was to get on with marrying Bea's father.

'Rose?' said Dante in her ear, 'are you still there?'

'Yes,' she said hastily.

'I thought I'd lost you. I shall contact Tony right now to confirm and will ring you again later. Or will you be too tired?'

'No. Ring me whatever time it is.'

He sighed. 'Ah, Rose, I wish I was there with you. It is strange that I have survived for years without you, yet now the wait to have you both here with me is intolerable.'

Both. Rose yearned for Dante to long for her alone for once, and felt mortified because she did. 'By the way, I've had some feelers about my business, but I'm going to wait for a while before putting the house up for sale.'

There was silence for a moment. '*Perche*? You feel the need of a sanctuary to run to if I do not make you happy?'

'No. It's just that the market is flat right now, so I'll wait until things improve.'

Dante sounded unconvinced as he said goodbye. Rose wished she hadn't mentioned the subject, and by the time he rang again later to report on his talk with Tony her headache was making her queasy.

'All is arranged, *cara*,' he told her. 'Tony and Allegra are very happy for us.'

'That's good.' Rose hesitated. 'Dante, are you upset because I'm keeping the house?'

He laughed. 'No, I am not. It is your house to do with as you wish. Now, let us talk of wedding dresses. Please allow me to pay for them, Rose.'

'Thank you, but no, Dante. Mum insists on footing the bill for the bride—*and* the bridesmaid.'

When the wedding day finally came—though at one stage Rose had been convinced it never would—she felt a sense of *déjà vu* as she entered the Hermitage. But today she was the one holding Tom's arm, and of the two strikingly handsome Italian men waiting for her, this time round Dante Fortinari was the bridegroom. *Her* bridegroom.

At first sight of the smiling faces turned towards her in the private room used for the ceremony, Rose's heart filled with such mixed emotions she felt giddy and held on tightly to the small hand of the bridesmaid, who grew very excited when she spotted assorted cousins waving at her.

'Look, Mummy,' Bea said, waving back, then beamed. 'And there's Daddy with Uncle Fabio.'

Dante watched the progress of the bride and bridesmaid with pride blazing in his eyes. He received Rose from Tom with murmured thanks and kissed his daughter lovingly before Tom bore her off to sit with Grace and Charlotte.

Dante made the simple vows with such passionate sincerity Rose had to fight against tears as she responded, hardly able to believe this was really happening at last as Dante drew his bride's hand through his arm afterwards to walk past the rows of smiling guests.

'Who is the fair man with Leo and Harriet?' asked Rose.

'Pascal Tavernier, my cousin's husband. Rosa is not here, much to her wrath, because she is about to give birth. Her absence will save much confusion. She is only distantly related to Harriet, but so strongly resembles her she could be her twin.'

'She must be very beautiful then,' said Rose.

'*Certo*, but not as beautiful as my wife,' said Dante in a tone which transformed Rose into the quintessential blushing bride as their daughter came running to join them in a flurry of organdie frills, the chaplet of flowers still miraculously anchored to her curls as she linked hands with her parents and beamed for the photographers.

Among the festive gold and silver balloons in the Hermitage ballroom, Rose could hardly believe this was happening as she stood with Dante to receive their guests in almost exactly the same places they'd occupied years before at Charlotte's wedding. Something Charlotte was quick to point out while Grace and Tom, and then Maria and Lorenzo Fortinari hugged and kissed the bride and groom.

'I am so happy,' said Maria, dabbing carefully at her eyes. 'You look so lovely, Rose—and so does our little angel.' She bent to kiss Bea. 'That is such a beautiful dress, *bella*.'

'I choosed it myself,' said Bea happily, and tugged on Grace's hand. 'This is my gramma, *Nonna*.'

Maria kissed Grace, and then smiled up at Tom and kissed him, too. 'Now we are all family, *tesoro*,' she informed her granddaughter.

After so much hugging and kissing, Rose left

her daughter with her two grandmothers and went off with Harriet and Charlotte before the meal to make repairs.

'That's a very clever dress,' said Harriet as Rose straightened the folds of chiffon.

'More clever than you know,' said Charlotte. 'It's a replica of the one she wore as my brides-maid. How on earth did you find it, love?'

Rose smiled. 'I was lucky enough to find the right shade of fabric and a dressmaker willing to copy the dress in the photograph.'

'From his reaction when he saw you, Dante be-lieves he's the lucky one,' said Harriet.

'That's because I come part of a package with our daughter,' said Rose, smiling as Allegra Mostyn put her pretty freckled face round the door.

'Get a move on, Signora Fortinari—the bride, not you, Harriet. Dante's getting impatient out there.'

'Coming,' said Rose, surprised as Harriet gave her a fierce hug.

'You are so wrong, Rose. Make no mistake, Dante's in seventh heaven because he's finally got *you*. So off you go, sister-in-law. A wedding day goes by fast—enjoy every minute of it while you can!'

Charlotte smiled triumphantly. 'And today you're the bride, not the bridesmaid.'

Still finding this part hard to believe, Rose held out her arms as Grace joined them to kiss her daughter tenderly, her eyes bright with unshed tears beneath the spectacular hat Tom had bought for her. 'Are you enjoying your day, my darling?'

Rose nodded and hugged her tightly. 'Thank you so very much, Mum.'

'What for?'

'Everything.'

Dante was waiting impatiently in the lobby as the others hurried on their way to let the bride and groom make their triumphal entry. 'You look so beautiful, *tesoro*,' he told Rose, his eyes glowing. 'And so like the girl at the Vilari wedding I thought I was dreaming when you walked towards me today.'

'You like my dress?'

'So much I cannot wait to take it off,' he said in her ear, then laughed delightedly at her heightened colour and took her hand as music struck up inside the ballroom to herald the arrival of the bride and groom. '*Allora*. That is our song!'

Later that evening, when they were finally alone in one of the luxury suites at the Chesterton in town, Dante took his bride in his arms and kissed her with a sigh of relief. 'At last I have you to myself, Signora Fortinari.'

Rose smiled wryly. 'Is that really me?'

He nodded and rubbed his cheek against hers. 'It is a title you share with my mother, also with Harriet, so, to be sure you know who you belong to, *sposa mia*, think of yourself as Signora Dante Fortinari.'

'I will,' she assured him and hesitated, wondering whether to give him her news now. No. Best to keep it for later. 'It was such a lovely day, Dante.' She turned her back. 'I should have changed before we left the Hermitage but—'

'You knew I would want to take the dress off myself,' he agreed, and kissed the nape of her neck. *'Mille grazie, tesoro.'*

'You're welcome! Will you undo my buttons, please?'

Dante heaved in a deep breath. '*Dio*, Rose, my hands are unsteady and you have many buttons.'

'Exactly the same number as last time.'

'I do not remember undoing so many!'

'You didn't undo any.' Rose turned her head to meet his eyes. 'I was so eager I did it myself.'

Dante breathed in sharply and buried his face against her neck. 'This time,' he said through his teeth, 'even though I want you more than my next breath, *I* will do it, *innamorata.'* He began undoing the tiny satin-covered buttons with speed and dexterity which quickly sent the dress into a heap of caramel chiffon at Rose's feet, and he snatched her up in his arms and carried her to the bed, his eyes dancing as he saw the blue silk garter above one knee.

'My something blue,' she said breathlessly.

Dante slid the garter down her leg and took it off to put in his pocket, then, with maddeningly slow care, removed her stockings and the satin underwear that had cost almost as much as her dress. He looked at her in simmering silence for a moment and then, careless of finest designer tailoring, tore off the rest of his clothes. He pulled her to her feet beside the bed to hold her close and kissed her parted mouth. 'I want you so much, Rose,' he whispered.

Not exactly what she wanted to hear, but for now it was enough because she wanted him just as much.

He bent to pull back the covers on the bed. 'I can wait no longer, *sposa mia*.' He picked her up and gave a purring growl of pleasure as they came together in the bed, skin to skin.

Rose melted against him, luxuriating in contact with the lean, muscular body that to her eyes could have been a model for one of the sculptures she'd seen in Florence. When she told him this between kisses Dante stared at her in astonishment for a moment, then saw by the look in her eyes that she meant every word and kissed her hard on her parted, eager mouth before his lips joined with his seeking hands in a glissando of caresses that transformed her entire body into a trembling erogenous zone.

'I know it sounds silly,' she gasped, 'but this feels new, as though we'd never made love before.'

'We have not done so for an entire endless month, and never as man and wife,' he whispered, and positioned his taut, aroused body between her thighs. 'Now, *tesoro*!'

Rose clasped Dante close, her inner muscles

caressing the hard length of him as he thrust home into her welcoming heat. He kissed her endlessly, murmuring passionate loving words into her ear as his caressing hands and demanding body drew such a wild response. As he possessed her she stifled a scream when the almost unbearable rapture of her orgasm overwhelmed her a second or two before Dante gave a triumphant groan and surrendered to his own.

They lay together afterwards in a boneless tangle of arms and legs, Dante's face buried in her hair.

'A good thing the other guests are all staying at the Hermitage,' said Rose at last. 'Sorry I was so noisy, Dante.'

He raised his head, his eyes blazing down into hers with pride. 'It is the greatest compliment you could pay me, *tesoro*. I feel like a king to know I gave you pleasure!'

'Did I give *you* pleasure?'

'Pleasure,' he said with feeling, 'is not a big enough word. I have made love to other women in my life. You know that. But with you there is rapture I have never experienced before.' He frowned. 'You are crying, *tesoro*?'

She sniffed hard. 'That was such a beautiful thing to say, Dante.' But still not quite the words she longed to hear.

'It is the truth,' he assured her and with a sigh of contentment turned on his back to pull her close. 'I hope our little angel sleeps well tonight.'

To her shame, Rose's pleasure dimmed a little after Dante's attention reverted so swiftly to his daughter. 'Since she's safe in Tom's house with my mother, and Charlotte and Fabio are there, too, Bea will be fine.' She smiled up into his relaxed, handsome face as she stroked the slim, strong hand now adorned with a wedding ring, something, he'd informed her, he'd refused to wear during his former marriage. 'It's time I let you into a little secret. Everyone thinks I named her Beatrice for my grandmother, and in one way this is true, but it was also my own private little joke.'

'Joke?' Dante looked down at her in question.

'Beatrice was the love of your poet, Dante Alighieri, so I named my baby for her as my secret connection to you.'

A look of pain swept over his face. 'Ah, Rose, if I had known!'

'If you had you couldn't have done anything

about it at the time, but I thought you'd like to know now we're married.'

'I do like it very much.' He raised her hand to his lips. 'It is much happier than the revelation given to me on my first wedding night.'

Rose took in a deep breath. 'Talking of revelations, I've been waiting for the right moment to give you another one.'

'You have a buyer for the house?'

'No, something far more important than that.' She propped herself on one elbow to look into his face. 'We're going to have another baby, Dante. It must have happened the night you came back after our quarrel...' Her voice trailed away as he shot upright, eyes narrowed as they speared hers. He gazed at her in silence for so long Rose felt cold. 'Say *something*, Dante, please!'

'So,' he said heavily, 'this is why you agree to marry me. You had many doubts about giving up your independence and your home and job here in England, then suddenly you say yes and I do not question it. I thought you had changed your mind because, like a fool, I believed you wanted me.' His mouth twisted. 'But it was only because you were *incinta* again.'

'No, Dante, that's not true, or at least not totally. I'll admit that it was the final, deciding factor.' She flushed miserably. 'I already had one father-less child. It was a shock to find I was about to produce another.'

'Neither child is fatherless,' he snapped. 'They are both mine. But why did you not tell me until now? Were you afraid I would cancel the wed-ding? You think I could do such a thing to Bea?' Dante flung out of bed to make for the bathroom.

Just once, thought Rose bitterly, it would have been good for Dante to think of her first, before Bea. Petty it might be, but on this particular night it would have been the perfect wedding gift.

Her nudity suddenly embarrassing, Rose opened the suitcase sitting at the foot of the bed and got into the ivory silk nightgown Charlotte had given her. She wrapped herself in the matching dress-ing gown and tied the sash tightly, wincing as her headache suddenly returned in full force. She should have kept her secret to herself, at least for tonight. With a sigh, she perched on the edge of the bed to wait. When Dante finally came out wearing one of the hotel bath robes, he sat beside her, leaving a space between them, she noted with a sinking heart.

'So, Rose,' he demanded, his voice stern, 'I ask again. Why did you not tell me sooner?'

Suddenly furious, she shot him a flaying look. 'Because I was naïve enough to keep the news as a wedding present to you—a sort of consolation prize to make up for your previous wedding night. So if anyone's a fool, Dante, it's me!' She jumped up and marched into the bathroom, then slammed the bolt home on the door.

'*Rose!*' ordered Dante hotly. 'Come back to me. Now!'

Rose gulped, feeling first hot then icy cold as she dropped to her knees and parted with what little wedding breakfast she'd eaten. Tears poured down her face as she cursed the fate which scheduled her first bout of morning sickness for tonight of all nights. Shivering and miserable, she ignored the banging on the door until Dante threatened to break it down.

'*Dio*, Rose!' he exclaimed when she staggered to her feet to let him in. He stared in horror at her ashen, sweating face. 'What is wrong?'

'What could possibly be wrong?' she flung at

him. 'I've been sick, I'm pregnant again and, just like the first time, I don't want to be. Go away!' she spat in desperation, but Dante ignored her. He mopped her gently with a damp facecloth and picked her up to carry her back to bed.

He laid her down gently. 'Lie very still, Rose.' He took her hand. 'What can I do for you? Would you like water, or I can ring for tea—'

'You don't have to.'

'Of course I have to,' he said roughly, his grasp tightening.

'I meant,' she said wearily, 'that you needn't ring for room service. There's a tea tray with a kettle and so on over on the table by the sofa. You can make the tea for me.'

The relief in Dante's eyes was so gratifying she warmed towards him slightly.

'You will trust me to make it correctly, Rose?'

'Yes. But not yet. I'll have a glass of water first, please.'

Dante helped her to sit up, then piled pillows behind her and settled her against them with care. 'You feel better now?'

Rose nodded. 'Yes, thank you.'

His lips tightened. 'You need not thank me so politely. I am happy to do anything to help you.'

Except tell her he loved her. 'I'll have that water now, then.'

'*Subito!*' Dante said promptly. He filled a glass with mineral water and sat on the bed beside her, watching her sip very slowly. 'You have been suffering much with *la nausea*, Rose?'

'No. This is the first time tonight.' She pulled a face and put the half-empty glass on the bedside table. 'Bad move to get morning sickness on our wedding night.'

Dante winced. 'I think perhaps it was I who made you ill, not our baby.'

Slightly mollified when he said 'our baby', Rose shrugged. 'Possibly. Your reaction to my news wasn't *quite* the one I expected.'

'*Mi dispiace!*' he said and took her hand. 'Coming so soon after experiencing such rapture together, I was not thinking clearly.'

'You sounded pretty clear on the subject to me. But let's not talk about it any more. Perhaps you could make that tea for me now?'

Dante got up at once and crossed the room to switch on the kettle. '*Allora,*' he said, 'I pour the boiling water on the tea bag, leave it for a little while, then remove the bag and add a little milk. Yes?'

Rose nodded. 'Exactly right.'

'Bene.' Dante went through the process with care and finally brought a steaming cup over to Rose.

'Thank you.' She eyed him over it. 'Not quite the wedding night you'd hoped for, is it?'

He gestured towards the sofa under the window. 'You would prefer me to sleep there tonight?'

'Of course not,' she retorted. 'I assume you intend me to share your room at the Villa Castiglione?'

Dante's eyes locked on hers. 'My room and my bed,' he stated in tones which left her in no doubt.

'Then we may as well start as we mean to go on. Besides,' she added, eyeing the sofa, 'you'll never fit on that.'

'Davvero! But I was happy to make the attempt tonight to let you rest.'

'Very noble, but no sacrifice required.' Rose slid carefully out of bed, stood for a moment to make sure she was steady on her feet, then made for the bathroom. 'Just give me five minutes to brush my teeth.'

When she got back Dante had tidied the bed and left only one lamp burning. He looked at her searchingly. 'Were you ill again?'

'No. I think that was a one-off just now—at least for tonight.' She untied her sash and slid the dressing gown off into his waiting hands. 'That bed looks very inviting,' she told him, suddenly almost too tired to speak as she slid into bed.

He drew the covers over her. 'I will be minutes only, Rose.'

It seemed like only seconds before Dante switched off the lamp and got in beside her. He hesitated for a moment, then lay flat on his back and took her hand. *'Buonanotte, sposa mia,'* he said softly.

'Good night, Dante.' Rose closed her eyes thankfully, well aware that he'd wanted to put his arms round her and hold her close, but had opted for hand-holding instead. Good move, she approved hazily. His unexpected reaction to her news had cut deep. Any attempt at cuddling by Dante right now would have met with short shrift.

CHAPTER TWELVE

THE RETURN TO the Villa Castiglione the next day was physically far less of an ordeal than Rose had expected. When she woke up she felt a moment of panic when she heard Dante in the bathroom, but then relaxed when she found that her digestive system was in good working order. No dash to the bathroom was necessary. When her new husband emerged, towelling his wet curls, he eyed her searchingly.

'*Buongiorno*, Rose. How do you feel today?'

'Good morning. I feel better, thank you.'

'No nausea?'

She gave it some thought. 'None at all.'

He relaxed visibly. '*Grazie a Dio*. You gave me much worry last night. But be truthful, Rose—are you well enough to travel today?'

'Yes, definitely.' Postponing the trip, even by a day, would mean explanations to her mother she would rather avoid right now. And a second round of goodbyes would be bad for Bea—and herself, if it came to that. Rose slid out of bed and stood up, shaking her head as he moved swiftly, ready to help her. 'I'm fine, Dante, really. After a shower I'll feel even better. What time do we leave?'

'At ten. I will order breakfast.' He put an arm round her. 'What would you like?'

'Just toast and tea, please.' She detached herself very deliberately. 'I won't be long.'

Dante stood back, his eyes sombre. 'You have not forgiven me.'

'Not yet, but I'm working on it.' Rose busied herself with choosing clothes to take into the bathroom with her.

'You are shy of dressing in front of me?' he demanded.

She turned in the bathroom doorway. 'Awkward, rather than shy. I'm not used to sharing my life with a man, Dante. You'll have to make allowances.'

He smiled crookedly. 'Then, to avoid further awkwardness for you, I will dress while you shower.'

'Thank you.' Rose closed the bathroom door and got to work, grateful to Dante for not pointing out that there had been no awkwardness last night when he was *un*dressing her. But today, illogically, it would have been hard to put her clothes on in front of him in the new intimacy of married life—which was something she had to get over pretty quickly to make that life successful, if only for Bea's sake. She patted her stomach gently. *For you, too*, she added. After all, compared with life as a single mother, she was living the dream as Dante's wife. His physical response to her, at least, was everything she could wish for. She would just have to work on changing that into the more cerebral love she felt for him. Not that hers was totally cerebral. Otherwise she wouldn't be expecting his second child. Whatever her brain felt about Dante, her hormones were utterly mad about him.

The limousine trip to the airport and the flight to Pisa went just as smoothly as the first time with Dante in charge. Worried beforehand that the nausea would return en route at some stage, Rose survived the entire flight without a qualm, and to reassure Dante even ate some of the meal.

As before, Tullio was waiting at the airport and

had taken time out of his Sunday to help them collect their luggage and hand over the car keys.

'*Congratulazione*, Signora Fortinari,' he said to Rose and kissed her hand then shook Dante's and congratulated him in turn.

'*Grazie*, Tullio,' she said, secretly thrilled to bits with her new title.

After a quick exchange with Tullio while he helped load their luggage into the waiting car, Dante helped Rose into the car and, with a quick wave for his assistant, joined the traffic leaving the airport.

'I will not drive fast,' Dante assured her, smiling, and Rose laughed.

'Unlike my—*our*—daughter, I don't mind fast!'

'Nevertheless, I have no wish to make you ill again, *carina*.' He gave her a sidelong glance. 'I asked Silvia to prepare the house and leave food for us, but then take a little holiday so we can begin our new life in peace together. But,' he added when Rose made no response, 'if you want her to come as usual I shall call her back.'

'Of course I don't. When Mum and Tom bring Bea to join us, peace will be hard to come by.'

She shot him a wry glance. 'Though I know you can hardly wait!'

He shook his head. 'Much as I love Bea, it will be good for us to have time alone together for a little while, Rose, yes?'

Yes, she rejoiced silently.

'And after a while perhaps you will not feel so awkward with me,' he said with a wry twist to his mouth.

'I'll do my best, Dante.'

'I do not doubt this,' he assured her, and smiled as he saw her eyelids droop.

'Sorry,' she said, yawning.

'Take the little nap, *bella*. I will wake you when we are near home.'

Home, thought Rose, closing her eyes. Not Willow House any more, but the Villa Castiglione. Her lips curved. It would be good to be alone there with Dante for a while…

She woke with a start to a screeching, crunching sound, her heart pounding as something hit the car. Cursing violently, Dante stood on the brakes and her head hit the side window with a crack that knocked her out for an instant.

Rose came round almost at once because Dante

was crushing her hand as he called her name in anguish, along with a flood of impassioned enquiries she couldn't understand.

'Answer me, Rose!' he demanded frantically. 'Where are you hurt?'

'Only my head,' she said groggily. 'What happened?'

'Some *bastardo* took a bend too fast and made contact with our front wing, then drove off like a maniac.' Dante leaned over her, his face haggard. '*Dio*, your head is bleeding. I must get you to a doctor immediately.'

'I don't need a doctor!'

'You do,' said Dante inexorably, and wiped her forehead with a handkerchief. 'Stay very still now while I arrange this.' He took out his phone and after a pause spoke to someone at length.

Rose listened to the rapid-fire conversation, but was unable to pick out more than the word *incinta*. At least she knew what that meant. It obviously had the desired effect, since Dante thanked someone volubly and turned to Rose. 'We will be seen immediately we arrive. I just need to check that the car is safe to drive then I will take you to the doctor. I will be seconds only.'

In sudden need of fresh air, Rose undid her belt and got out very carefully, relieved to find her legs steady as she watched Dante make a long examination under the bonnet. She whistled as she saw ugly scrapes along the shining crimson paint. 'How bad is it?'

'It is cosmetic only. The paintwork is scratched but there is no damage to the car otherwise.' He closed the bonnet. 'It is safe to drive, I promise. *Mi dispiace*, Rose. Even when I was young and drove very fast I never had an accident, yet today, when I was taking such care, this happened.'

'Only because some idiot was speeding. It wasn't your fault!'

'*Grazie, tesoro.* Does your head ache?'

'A bit. Do I look a mess?'

Dante pulled her close, his heart hammering against hers. 'You are still bleeding a little, but you are beautiful, as always.' He swallowed hard. 'When your head hit the window my heart stopped. It is good that *bastardo* drove off so fast,' he added, eyes blazing. 'I wanted to kill him.'

'Bad idea! I don't fancy visiting my new husband in prison.' She smiled. 'Thank heavens Bea wasn't with us.'

'Amen,' breathed Dante, and managed a smile. 'Though I was not driving fast!'

Rose chuckled then eyed him searchingly. 'Were you hurt anywhere, Dante?'

He shook his head. 'A few bruises and badly injured pride only. I am mortified that you had to experience such a thing, *carissima*.'

'I'll live. And so, in case you were wondering, will our baby.'

'That is good—but in that terrible moment when you hit your head I had no thought for the baby, only for you, that I might have lost you a second time, this time perhaps for ever.' He blinked hard, but tears, Rose noted in wonder, hung on his enviable lashes.

Oblivious of passing traffic, or anyone in the world who might be watching, she pulled her husband's head down to kiss him fiercely. 'Well, you haven't,' she said gruffly. 'I don't suppose you have a tissue?'

'This handkerchief only.' He gave it to her, his eyes smouldering. 'That was a wonderful kiss. Do it again.'

'Later,' she said. 'Spit!'

He laughed as he obliged, and held still while

she scrubbed a bloodstain from his cheek then gave him the handkerchief.

'Now you do the same for me.'

Once Dante was sure Rose felt composed enough to continue their journey he drove her to the private hospital used by the Fortinari family. As promised, they were seen immediately by a doctor who asked rapid questions Dante translated for Rose while the cut on her temple was dressed. When it was established that Signora Fortinari was not suffering from concussion, and a scan later confirmed that all else was otherwise well with her, the doctor told Dante he could take his wife home on condition that he brought her back immediately if she felt unwell.

When Dante finally drove up the winding road to the Villa later Rose gave a deep sigh of relief as the lovely old house came into view. 'Home at last,' she said thankfully.

'It is so good to hear you say *home*,' Dante said with feeling. He got out to help her out of the car, and then picked her up to carry her into the house. 'This is the custom for brides, yes?'

Rose wreathed her arms round his neck happily,

surprised when, instead of taking her into the *salone*, he carried her straight upstairs to their room and carefully laid her down on the pristine bed before casting himself face down beside her, breathing hard, his arm possessive across her waist.

She lay still for a while, but then patted his arm. 'I hate to spoil this romantic moment, Dante, but I'm hungry.'

'I also,' he agreed and sat up, smiling down at her. 'So tonight we will have a picnic up here from whatever Silvia has left for us. I will bring it and you do nothing except lie there and look beautiful.'

Her eyes sparkled. 'Oh, well, if you insist! But I'll have more chance of looking halfway beautiful if I can have a shower first, so could you bring up some of the luggage before you start on the picnic? And I'll ring Mum to report in and check on Bea.'

The euphoria of surviving what could well have been a serious accident cast a magical aura over their first evening together at the Villa as husband and wife. Dante, who prided himself on his driving skills, was obviously mortified about the incident, but Rose was deeply grateful for it. His anguished reaction when she was hurt had re-moved all her doubts about Dante's feelings. He had no need now to tell her he loved her. She knew.

When Dante returned after removing the re-mains of their picnic supper he raised an eyebrow as he asked why she was so deep in thought. Rose hesitated for a moment then made a clean breast of her doubts and fears, which won her a stare of utter amazement. 'You did not believe I love you?'

Rose tucked her hair behind her ears. 'You never actually said so, though I knew you wanted me, physically.'

'How could you not? At your slightest touch I am on fire, *amore*!' He sat down on the bed beside her and took her in his arms. 'But that is only part of my love for you, Rose. I want to spend every minute possible of the rest of my life with you, raise our children together, and grow old together. That is how I love you. Is it enough?'

She smiled at him through a sudden haze of tears and hugged him close. 'More than enough—even though you were so horrible to me on our wedding night.'

Dante winced and rubbed his cheek against

hers. 'Forgive me, *carissima*, but try to understand. I wanted you to love me as a husband and lover, and for a moment I thought you married me only to gain a father for another child.'

'While I was afraid that you took me on just to get Bea as part of the package,' said Rose, and grinned sheepishly at the incredulous look he gave her.

'How could you believe that? In Firenze I could not hide my delight at meeting you again. And I knew nothing about our child at that time.' Dante laid his forehead against hers. 'So, to avoid all future confusion, Signora Fortinari, I have loved you from the first day we met. *Ti amo, sposa mia.* Do you understand me?'

'I do, I do. So make sure you understand, too, Dante Fortinari. I married you for exactly the same reason.'

'For which I thank God.' Dante slid the dressing gown from her shoulders and tossed it away. 'You forgive me then, *innamorata*?'

She pretended to think it over. 'I'm working on it.'

Dante pulled her close. 'Always I am the peace-maker, in the business and with my family,' he

said bitterly. 'Unlike Leo, who can be abrasive—
that is right? I am the one who pours the oil on
the troubled waters. Yet on my wedding night I
accuse my bride of sins she has not committed.'

'True. You'll just have to spend the rest of our
honeymoon making it up to me,' she ordered.

'With much, much pleasure, *amore*! I have given
instructions to my family to leave us in peace at
the Villa Castiglione for a while when they return from England tomorrow.' Dante raised his
head to look down at her. 'They were surprised
that you did not want somewhere exotic for our
honeymoon.'

'I just wanted to start our life together at the
Villa without our little darling for a couple of
weeks.' Rose sighed as she stretched against him.
'You know, even with the marriage vows to prove
it, I can hardly believe that we're here together at
last, Dante.'

He drew her closer. 'To have you here in my
arms as my wife is a dream come true, *tesoro*.'

'I never dared to dream anything so unlikely!'
She smiled up at him. 'Even though the first day
we met I knew who you were before we were even
introduced.'

'I knew at first sight that you were the love of my life, *carissima*,' he said huskily. 'So who did you think I was?'

'The man of my dreams. But dreams were all I had for years, Dante.'

'Now we have the glorious reality, yes?'

'We certainly do. Shall I tell you something else, Dante?'

'Anything you wish *amore*.' His arms tightened. 'Will I like this something?'

Rose nodded and rubbed her cheek against his, which, she noted lovingly, was already showing signs of needing a shave. 'I used to tell myself that one day my prince would come, and now here he is at last, right here in my arms.'

'Where he intends to stay,' said Dante with emphasis and then shook his head. 'But I am no prince, *tesoro*.'

'You are in *my* fairy tale!'

He gave her the smile he shared with his child. 'And because I have read many fairy tales to our daughter I know exactly how they end—we live happily ever after!'

By the end of the fortnight, blissfully happy though her honeymoon had been, Rose was in a fever of excitement at the airport in Pisa as she saw her child running towards them with Grace in pursuit and Tom, laden with luggage, following behind.

There was a laughing collision as Rose seized her child, and Dante caught them both in his encircling arms and kissed his daughter's beaming face as she talked non-stop.

Rose gave Bea a smacking kiss and then hugged Grace. 'How's Gramma?'

'Doing fine,' her mother assured her. 'Bea was no trouble at all except for the odd tear when she realised she was missing you.' She turned to Tom. 'We enjoyed having her to ourselves, didn't we?'

Tom dumped down the luggage to kiss Rose. 'We had Charlotte and Fabio's help for the first week, but the rest of it was excellent practice for when the first little Vilari arrives.' He held out his hand to Dante, smiling. 'No need to ask how *you* are!'

'*Davvero,*' agreed Dante, surrendering Bea to her mother. 'I am a very lucky man. Welcome, Tom,' he added, picking up some of the luggage. 'The car is outside.'

Bea frowned as Dante fastened her into her

seat. 'I don't like this car, Daddy. I like your shiny red one.'

'It needed painting, so your Uncle Leo lent me this,' he said, kissing her nose. 'But this is your very own red car seat.'

Bea lay back in it like a queen on a throne with Rose and Grace close together beside her. 'Can we go and see Luca and Chiara tomorrow, Daddy?' she demanded.

'Possibly.' He exchanged a gleaming look with Rose over his shoulder. '*Andiamo*, let us go home.'

'Not fast!' warned Bea.

'No, *piccola*,' Dante assured her, laughing. 'I will not drive fast.'

Because he kept his word, Bea soon nodded off, leaving Rose to enjoy Grace's company.

'I've no need to ask how you are,' said her mother, squeezing her hand. 'You glow.'

'I enjoyed these two weeks alone with Dante,' Rose admitted. 'I missed Bea, naturally, but it was good to have time together before we get back to parenthood.'

Bea woke as Dante turned up the steep, winding road to the Villa. 'Gramma,' she said in excitement, 'Daddy's house is up here—ooh,' she squeaked in delight as he drove up through the garden. 'Balloons! Is there a party?' She jumped up and down in her seat. 'Look, Tom, Auntie Charlotte's on the loggia.'

'And not just Auntie Charlotte,' said Grace with misgiving, and grasped Rose's hand. 'Do I look all right?'

'You look gorgeous,' Tom assured her.

'Daddy, Daddy, get me out,' demanded Bea, as an assortment of cousins came streaming from the house. Dante unbuckled his impatient daughter and set her on her feet so she could run to join the youngsters who surrounded her, laughing, then delivered her onto the loggia into the embraces of her *Nonna* and *Nonno*. The senior Fortinaris gave Tom and Grace a warm welcome, smiling as a radiantly happy Charlotte kissed the new arrivals then handed them on to Fabio and Leo and Harriet, and finally to Mirella and Franco.

Rose hung back for a moment with Dante just to breathe in the noisy, laughing chaos of the scene. He put his arm round her, smiling down into her flushed face. 'You are happy, *amore*?'

'Yes,' she said simply. 'At this moment I have everything in the world I never dared wish for. A beautiful home, a loving, welcoming family, and my mother here with me to share it all today—but most of all, Dante, I have you.'

'Ah, *carissima*!' He took her in his arms and kissed her in passionate gratitude, a move which won much applause and laughter from the crowded loggia.

'Come, *mio figlio*,' said Maria Fortinari, smiling. 'Release your bride for a moment. She will want to show Grace and Tom to their room to do the freshening up, and then we eat, yes, Rose?'

A few minutes later everyone crowded round the table laid in the garden, the noise level high as they enjoyed the food Maria Fortinari and her cook had helped Silvia prepare.

Under cover of the joyful hubbub, Grace took Rose's hand. 'I've no need to ask if you're happy, love.'

Rose gave a deep, relishing sigh. 'I'll be even happier if you—and Tom, of course—promise to come and stay with us as often as you can.'

'I can safely promise that, especially when Charlotte's baby arrives—I won't be able to keep him away!' Grace looked up at the house. 'I'm so glad

I've seen your beautiful home. I'll be able to picture the three of you here.'

Rose eyed her husband in surprise as he got up to rap a spoon on his glass.

'Listen carefully, everyone, because I make my speech in English so Grace and Tom understand how happy I am to welcome them both here today and thank them for taking care of Bea these past two weeks.' At the mention of her name Bea left her place between Chiara and Luca and went running to her father. He picked her up and kissed her in a way which brought tears to his mother's eyes and to a few others round the table, notably Charlotte's.

'Hormones,' she apologised, blowing her nose into the handkerchief Fabio had ready.

'So now,' continued Dante, 'I wish to thank my mother-in-law for giving her daughter and her granddaughter into my keeping, also Tom, for taking such good care of Rose and Bea in the past.'

To Rose's surprise, Grace exchanged a look with Tom and got to her feet. 'Thank you, Dante, and everyone here for giving us this wonderful welcome. I shall go home—'

'Not yet, Grace,' called Charlotte.

'Not yet,' agreed Grace, smiling, 'but when I do I shall look back on today and feel happy because I know my girls are happy.'

'Davvero,' said Dante with feeling, and put his arm round Rose. 'After the years apart, it is now time we live happily ever after!'

'Like in my story book,' said Bea with satisfaction, and Dante laughed as he set her down.

'Only this is better because it is our story, yes?'

'Much better,' said Rose with feeling, and smiled all round to lighten the mood. 'Now, then, Harriet's made some gorgeous apple pies and I've made a very British trifle, so hands up. Who wants a *dolce*?'

* * * * *

Mills & Boon® Large Print
November 2014

CHRISTAKIS'S REBELLIOUS WIFE
Lynne Graham

AT NO MAN'S COMMAND
Melanie Milburne

CARRYING THE SHEIKH'S HEIR
Lynn Raye Harris

BOUND BY THE ITALIAN'S CONTRACT
Janette Kenny

DANTE'S UNEXPECTED LEGACY
Catherine George

A DEAL WITH DEMAKIS
Tara Pammi

THE ULTIMATE PLAYBOY
Maya Blake

HER IRRESISTIBLE PROTECTOR
Michelle Douglas

THE MAVERICK MILLIONAIRE
Alison Roberts

THE RETURN OF THE REBEL
Jennifer Faye

THE TYCOON AND THE WEDDING PLANNER
Kandy Shepherd

1014 Rom LP